ELLA'S LAST DANCE

Ballerinas

Sadie's Ballet School Dream
Luci in the Spotlight
Pippa on Pointe
Ella's Last Dance

Ballerinas
Ella's Last Dance

Harriet Castor

a division of Hodder Headline plc

First published in Great Britain in 1996
by Hodder Children's Books

10 9 8 7 6 5 4 3 2 1

A Catalogue record for this book is available from the British Library

ISBN 0 340 65132 6

Typeset by Avon Dataset Ltd, Bidford-on-Avon, Warks

Printed and bound in Great Britain by
Cox & Wyman, Reading, Berks

Hodder Children's Books
a division of Hodder Headline plc
338 Euston Road
London NW1 3BH

For Emily Davies, my god-daughter

Part One

Happy News?

One

'Hey, Arnold – look at this gorgeous little girl! She must be the granddaughter or something.'

The American woman smiled at me as I slowly made my way towards her table. The tray in my hands had Nonna's coffee pot and best cups on it, so I didn't dare hurry.

'Look at her wonderful Italian colouring!' she added, holding out her hands to take the tray from me. 'And she's such a graceful little thing. "A natural", Bernard would say–'

'Christine.' The man frowned.

'What? She can't understand me, Arnold.'

I rearranged the crockery on the little table between them to make room for the pot and cups. Then I pointed to the small wicker basket.

'Would you like some more bread?' I asked politely.

The woman's mouth dropped open – it looked ever so funny.

'What did I tell you, Christine?' muttered the man

under his breath. Then, seeing that his wife was still in shock, he answered my question. 'Er – no, thank you, my dear.'

I turned to go, but before I'd taken two steps, the woman spoke to me again.

'That's an excellent accent,' she said, really slowly and loudly as if I was deaf. 'You taking English class at school, honey?'

I shook my head. 'I live in Britain. I'm just staying with my grandmother for the holidays.'

'Ah.' The woman nodded, taking this in.

She didn't seem to want to say anything else, and I still had the empty bread basket in my hands, so I took it back to the kitchen.

There I found Nonna, in her big black skirt and woollen shawl, with her grey hair curled in a wide bun on her neck. She smiled when she saw me, as she always does.

'Good girl,' she said in Italian.

'What shall I do next?' I asked her.

Nonna took my face in her hands and kissed my forehead. 'Run along outside and play,' she said. 'You've done enough for one morning.'

I nodded. I understand a lot more Italian than I can speak. And, though Nonna says she's too old to learn English, between us, she and I manage pretty well.

I pushed on the wooden kitchen door and went outside into the morning sunshine.

Nonna's house is set apart from the rest of the

village, a little way along the narrow road that winds up the hillside. From her garden at the back of the house, you can see a long way, across the red-tiled rooftops, to the stone bell tower of the village church, and the fields beyond.

This morning the sun was warm, but not yet really hot – that would come in the middle of the day. These cooler hours were my favourite time, and every morning, after I'd helped serve Nonna's guests their breakfast, I would come out here to do my ballet practice.

At the far end of the garden, there was a tree whose lower branches scooped quite close to the ground – and one branch was exactly the right height to rest my hands on, like a barre. I stood in front of it now, with my heels placed together and my toes turned outwards, in first position, and started on my *pliés*.

'And bend . . . and stretch . . . keep your back straight . . .'

In my head, I could hear the voice of Miss Latimer, my ballet teacher. It made my mind drift back to my school in England – The Evanova School of Ballet. How Miss Latimer and all my friends there would laugh at the idea of morning class out on an Italian hillside!

'Arnold! There she is!'

I heard footsteps behind me on the dusty path that ran up from the house.

'And look – I told you. Such poise!'

When I turned, the American woman was picking

her way towards me, her reluctant husband in tow.

'Sorry to disturb you, honey!' she called as she came near, with a beaming smile shining from behind her large round glasses. 'But I just wanted to ask – do you take dancing lessons? You know – ballet?'

She said it 'ball-*ay*', not like English people do.

I nodded.

The woman turned to her husband. 'She does, Arnold,' she said, as if he wouldn't have seen my reply. Then she looked at me again. 'Where? Which school? If you don't mind my asking.'

'The Evanova School,' I said shyly.

'Oh – the Evanova!' The woman looked impressed. 'That's real famous, even in the States!'

I nodded again and smiled. I didn't quite know what to say.

'You see, my brother—' the woman began, but then her husband cut in.

'Come on, Christine. Leave the little girl alone. I'm sure she doesn't want to know.'

'Oh. Well.' The woman nodded and smiled at me again. 'My whole family's really into the ball-*ay*. None of us are dancers, you understand. But—' Her husband tugged at her sleeve. She shook him off, and held her hand out to me. 'I'm Christine Schindenberg Weller,' she said. 'And this is my husband, Arnold Weller.'

I shook hands with both of them. 'Gabriella Bruni,' I said. 'Pleased to meet you.'

The woman nodded. 'Well, we're off now – pushing

on to Florence. But good luck! I'm sure you'll make a fabulous dancer!'

'Thank you,' I said. The woman waved at me as she and her husband headed down the path again. I waved back.

Five minutes later, I watched as their car drove slowly down the road towards the village, kicking up clouds of dust behind it.

Two

The next Friday my eldest brother, Gianni, met me at Edinburgh airport.

'Ciao, bambina,' he said, taking my case and giving me a quick hug. 'You're brown as a nut. Had a good time with Nonna?'

I nodded. 'Brilliant!' Already, the holiday seemed like a dream. If I hadn't had the fresh panettone cake Nonna had baked me that morning carefully wrapped up in my bag, I might have thought I'd imagined the whole trip. The bustle of Edinburgh felt so very far away from the quiet of Nonna's hillside.

Soon we were in the car and heading across town. Gianni was telling me the latest news from my mum and dad's café and delicatessen.

'. . . so now Marinelli's place is opening for lunches too, and business has really dropped for us,' Gianni was saying. He talks really fast – like a horse-racing commentator, Mamma says. 'Papa's thinking about turning the back half of the café – you know, just beyond the archway – into a proper restaurant. So – if we start working evenings too, when are me and Lorenzo going to get any time off? You got it – never!'

He pulled up at some traffic lights and, pushing his sunglasses up on to his forehead, he glanced across at me. It must have been pretty obvious I'd hardly been listening to a word he'd said. He laughed. 'Didn't want to come home, then, huh?'

'Uh? Oh,' I shook my head. 'No . . . I mean, yes – in a way. I'm really looking forward to going back to school. I've missed my friends.'

'She doesn't miss her family, but she misses her friends!' teased Gianni, shaking his head. 'Who are these friends, then? You've not told me about them.'

You haven't asked, I could have said. I've been away at the Evanova School for two terms now, but Gianni is never interested in hearing about it when I come home for the holidays. He thinks ballet is boring. He's only interested in cars and football and girls – girls his own age, that is. Oh, and he's interested in the café and the shop of course, but only because he and Lorenzo – that's my other brother – have to work there.

'Well,' I pictured my three best friends in my head. 'There's Pippa, who I share a room with–'

'There are just two of you to a room?' Gianni interrupted. 'I thought these English boarding schools had – what do you call them? Dorms.'

'Dormitories,' I said. 'And no – this one doesn't. At least, the girls don't. We share in twos or threes. But the boys have dormitories. They live on the opposite side of the school to us–'

'Glad to hear it!'

'So, anyway – I share with Pippa. She's the daughter of a famous ballerina. Well, an ex-ballerina, actually. Called–'

'Is she pretty?'

'Pippa's mother?'

'No – Pippa, stupid!'

That was always Gianni's first question about any girl. If girls weren't pretty, Gianni wasn't interested in them. Luckily, he thought I was pretty – but that was probably just family loyalty!

Now I thought about Pippa. 'Yes, she is,' I said. 'She's got blonde hair and blue eyes. Oh, and long legs–'

'Sounds good,' said Gianni approvingly.

'Gianni! She's the same age as me!'

Gianni shrugged. 'So? I'll wait a few years,' he said, and gave a wolfish grin.

I sighed hotly, to show him how ridiculous I thought he was. Then I went on, 'Next there's Luci. She's Australian – but her family lives in London now. She's got really curly hair and freckles, and she bounces all over the place.'

'Freckles.' Gianna shook his head. 'I don't like freckles.'

'Last there's Sadie,' I said. 'Sadie and Luci have a room just along the corridor from the one Pippa and I share. Sadie's really nice. She's got pale skin, with sort of mid-brown hair. She hasn't done ballet for very long but she's ever so–'

'No,' Gianni flicked his sunglasses back on to his nose. 'I'll stick with this . . . Pippa, was it? The blonde, long-legged one.'

I giggled. I could just imagine Pippa looking down

her nose at my brother in her proud way. She could manage it, even though she's loads smaller than Gianni – Pippa can look down her nose at anyone!

'I think Mamma's right . . . pass the bread, will you, Ella?'

I reached for it. Lorenzo tore a chunk off without looking at me, and carried on.

'Taking on someone else just costs money and money's the problem in the first place, so what's the point?'

'The point?' Across the table, Papa flung down his fork. 'The point is that opening in the evenings will be a disaster without more staff! I'm telling you!'

He leant forward. The lamp, hanging low over the kitchen table, showed up beads of sweat on his forehead. 'Have you seen how many staff Marinelli has taken on? It's no use being some poor relation. To compete, we must beat them – we must be the best!'

'I know, but look –' Lorenzo shovelled another forkful of food into his mouth, chewed quickly, and swallowed. 'There's you and Mamma in the kitchen, right? – And there's me and Gianni waiting at tables. Be realistic. How many covers are we going to have? Not many – we just haven't the room–'

'Your mother and me in the kitchen? Oh, yes?' Papa spread his hands. 'And what are we going to do when the baby comes, huh?'

Suddenly, there was a thick silence. My mum looked

stunned, like she'd just been slapped in the face. Papa had his eyes fixed on me, and so did Gianni and Lorenzo. I didn't understand. What were they talking about? Why were they looking at me?

'Oh, Ella.' Mamma held her hand out. 'I didn't mean to tell you like this.' She drew me off my chair and round the corner of the table to sit on her knee.

'What is it?' I whispered, looking into her face.

She took one of my hands and pressed its palm to her tummy.

'A little brother or sister for you,' said Mamma, with this funny half happy, half sad look in her eyes.

I wanted to say something, but I couldn't. My brain had gone numb – as if I had a lump of ice-cream inside my head, freezing up all my thoughts. I just stared at Mamma in shock, and swallowed. Behind me, I heard the scrape of knives and forks on plates as Gianni and Lorenzo started eating again.

Mamma put her arms round me tightly, so my face got squashed against her shoulder, and rocked me back and forth, like she used to when I was little.

After a few minutes, I said into her shoulder – 'When will the baby come?'

'December, princess,' I heard Papa say behind me.

At last Mamma stopped rocking and gently held me away from her so she could see my face.

'We didn't plan for it to be like this, Ella,' she said. 'But it's happy news, isn't it?' She didn't look so sure of this herself, but I nodded, and she smiled. She rubbed my cheek with her thumb, as if testing how smooth my skin was. Then she helped me down from her knee and I went back to my own chair.

I still felt numb. It *was* happy news – people are always happy about new babies, aren't they? Then why didn't I feel happy? And why weren't Mamma and Papa acting happy either?

Lorenzo had finished his dinner now, and was leaning back in his chair, staring unconcernedly at the ceiling. Gianni was still eating. Papa was gazing into space. The line between his eyebrows looked deeper than usual.

'There's only one thing, princess,' he said, still not focussing on anything in particular. 'Something we have to talk to you about.'

Under the table, I hooked my feet around the legs of my chair.

'The café,' said Papa. 'It hasn't been doing so well.'

'I know.' I nodded. Ever since I'd got home this morning, that's all I'd heard anyone talking about.

'And the new baby will cost money,' said Mamma. 'Clothes, food – and that pram we had for you we gave to Gina, remember? We'll have to get another. We're pushed enough as it is – and you know how hard we're all working at the moment . . .'

I nodded again. Even Gianni and Lorenzo were looking tired. And I'd only been able to go to Italy this Easter because Nonna had had lots of guests and had saved up enough to send a bit of money to help with the plane fare.

'So I'm afraid, Ella,' Papa was saying, 'we just won't

be able to afford your fees for The Evanova School after this term.'

I frowned. 'So – who's going to pay them instead?'

I looked at Papa, then at Mamma. They stared back at me glumly.

'You don't mean –' I blurted, suddenly panicking, 'you don't mean I'll have to *leave*?'

I was still sitting on the same chair. It was the same table in front of me, with the same dinner on it. But it felt like the world had slipped before my eyes and now everything was out of place.

To think – just a few hours ago I'd been dreaming happily about school, about my friends, Sadie, Pippa and Luci . . .

'Ella? Ella!' Mamma was tugging at my hands. She seemed to be miles away, as if I was in a dream. 'Look,' she said, 'I'm going to write to your headmistress, and see if there isn't some sort of scholarship they give to pupils in this situation. Your reports have been excellent all year. I'm sure–'

'We'll sort it out, princess,' said Papa quickly.

'How?' I blurted. 'What if there *isn't* a scholarship? They told us there weren't any when I first got in. What if nothing's changed?'

There was no answer to that. Mamma and Papa exchanged a look.

I couldn't bear it any more. I felt a torrent of tears building up inside me – but there was no way I was going to cry in front of my brothers. I slid off my chair and ran from the room.

Outside, the twilight was rapidly thickening into darkness, but I didn't care. I pushed on down our long narrow garden, wading through the overgrown grass, and didn't stop till I got right to the end.

There was an old bench there, covered in grey lichen, and almost completely cut off from the rest of the garden by the straggling bushes and weeds. It was my private place to sit and think. Now I curled up there, hugging my knees tightly to my chest, and burst into tears. I hated this baby – I hated it already. Why couldn't someone wave a magic wand and make it go away? Why had everything suddenly gone wrong?

Three

'Ella!'

There was the rustle and crunch of someone making their way down the garden. I suddenly realised it was a lot darker than I'd thought; how long had I been sitting there?'

'Ella!'

Hurriedly I wiped my cheeks. 'Here, Gianni!'

The black shape of the bush in front of me quivered, and then was pushed to one side. Dipping his head to avoid the hanging branches of the willow, Gianni stepped into the little clearing.

'What are you doing?' He stood and looked at me.

I shrugged. 'Just thinking.'

'Thinking,' he echoed me sardonically. 'Mamma and Papa have enough to worry about right now.'

'I know.'

'So why are you sitting out here, then?' Gianni sat down beside me on the bench. 'Look – I know you're upset. You like this ballet school, right? You've got your friends, you get to prance about all day–'

'It's more than that! I'm going to be a dancer!'

Gianni sighed heavily. 'We've all got dreams, Ella. Do you think I want to work in a shop all my life? Right now, we're lucky to have a roof over our heads.'

I looked at him sharply. 'Is it really that bad?'

Gianni nodded. 'Papa doesn't tell me much. But I've never seen him look so worried. He's trying not to show it –' He hesitated, then turned to me gravely. 'Don't make it worse for them, OK? *OK*?'

I nodded.

'Dancers have to act – to tell a story, right?' said Gianni, more brightly.

'Right.'

'So – practise your acting now. Feeling lousy? Keep it to yourself. Because I can guarantee you one thing – however bad you're feeling, Papa and Mamma are feeling worse.'

Gianni put his arm round my shoulders and squeezed. 'Now, get yourself back inside. It's getting cold.'

Obediently, I stood up.

'Ella?'

I turned. Gianni put out a hand and ruffled my hair. 'When Gianni's rich, he'll buy you all the ballet lessons you want, yes?'

It was the sort of thing he used to say to me when I was little – when my big brothers seemed like storybook heroes to me, and I believed they really would make their fortunes one day.

Now, though, I knew that things didn't work out that way. And that by the time Gianni could afford to pay for my lessons, it would be too late. But I played along with it. 'Yes,' I said, trying to sound pleased, and surprised at how easily I could make my voice lie. Then I turned from him again and trudged back up the garden.

* * *

I did make an effort after that, I really did. All evening I tried to smile at my mum and dad and think of chatty things to say. It was hard – my head was so full of worries about school and the baby, that I had to rack my brains to try and think of other topics to talk about.

By the time I got to my bedroom, I was exhausted. I felt like I'd been holding my breath.

I changed carefully into my pyjamas, folding my day clothes neatly and putting them in my chest of drawers. Then I pulled back the sheets and climbed into bed. I put off the light straight away and, hooking back the edge of the curtain hanging beside me, I stared up at the night sky.

I was still lying there, wide awake, when I heard footsteps on the stairs. The bathroom door opened and closed several times, the landing light went off, and I heard the murmur of my parents' voices in the room next door.

They talked for a long time. Then, at last, they were quiet.

In the dark, my eyes were open. I knew I wouldn't sleep. I didn't even particularly want to. I was thinking back over all the years of once-a-week ballet lessons I'd had – years of dreaming of going to a full-time school, where everyone loved ballet as much as me, and where they really did train you to become a proper dancer one day.

Then, just last year, I had the chance to audition for the Evanova – and I got in. My dream came true, and for two whole terms I was so happy. Now I almost wished I'd never gone there at all: now I knew what I would be missing.

Part Two

Hopes and Fears

Four

As the minibus turned into the treelined driveway, I could hear a tune in my head. A beautiful, sad tune – one of the most famous pieces of ballet music in the world: The Swan, it's called, though the ballerina's solo that goes with it is called The Dying Swan.

As the gentle notes rose and fell, even the sight of the towering red-brick school building – the sight that usually makes my heart leap with excitement – seemed suddenly a melancholy one. Was this the last time I would start a new term as a pupil here? I couldn't bear the thought.

Along with the other pupils who'd been picked up at Wittingham station, I got off the school minibus and waited for the driver to open the big hatch where our luggage was stashed. The sky, which had been a clear delicate blue when my train had got in, had clouded over now, and a thin warmish drizzle had started to fall.

I just had one case, but it was heavy with dancing

shoes and school books, and it was a slow staggering progress I made up to the big wooden school door, across the entrance hall and along the passageway to the wide spiral staircase that led up to C corridor.

When at last I reached the door of the little bedroom I'd shared with Pippa since our very first day here last September, I paused, and stared at the name cards pinned there.

C19
GABRIELLA BRUNI
PIPPA JAMES

What would they say next term? Pippa and who else? The thought brought a lump to my throat. I swallowed, and prepared a smile on my face. Then I went in.

But the room was empty. And when I knocked on the door of C15, a short way back down the corridor, there was no reply. I was the first of our little gang to arrive. I went back to my room, sat on my bed in the greying afternoon light and stared absently through the window. I couldn't even bring myself to unpack.

Later in the afternoon, when the others had arrived, Luci and Sadie joined me in my bedroom to catch up on all the news. Pippa had gone to see Miss Lum, our matron, about her bedside light, which wasn't working.

'So he'll be on location in Idaho for three months, and then at the studios in Hollywood!' said Luci.

'Hollywood! Wow!' Sadie's face was a perfect picture of awed amazement.

'I know,' Luci beamed. 'His agent says he's really hit the big time!'

'My parents are so unexciting,' sighed Sadie. 'Compared to yours, I mean. What with Pippa and her famous ballerina mother, and now your step-dad, Luci, who's going to be winning an Oscar the next thing we know, I feel like my family's so drab. Know what I mean, Ella?' She nudged me teasingly.

'Oh – yes –' I tried to smile. I had a feeling it was a pathetic effort.

Sadie looked at me with a fleeting frown of concern. 'Ella – how was your Easter, then? I bet Italy was great, wasn't it? You've got a gorgeous tan.'

I shrugged and mumbled thanks for the compliment. I wouldn't tell them. I'd decided I wouldn't. Not yet. I . . .

'I've just heard the most amazing piece of news!' The door banged open and Pippa flew into the room. She knelt up on her bed, opposite mine, her eyes shining.

'Well?' Luci urged.

Pippa opened her mouth – then suddenly turned round to the door and, seeing that she'd left it wide open, she scrambled up to shut it carefully.

'Four people,' she said dramatically, looking round at us, 'got letters over the holidays. Telling them the teachers didn't think they'd progressed well enough in their dancing this year – so they wouldn't be invited back after the summer holidays!'

I put one hand to my mouth. I was stunned. Pippa

had delivered this news as if it was something exciting – but it was awful! I could see that Sadie was as shocked as me.

'Well?' Pippa frowned in frustration. 'Aren't you going to ask me who the people are?'

'Jeepers, so what the second years said was true!' said Luci, frowning. 'About the teachers watching us really carefully last term – assessing us and all that.' She leant forward. 'Hey – you're dead lucky, Pips. What with being injured last term and missing all those classes. Unless–' She stopped, wide-eyed. 'One of them, Pips, one of them wasn't you, was it?'

'No!' Pippa looked at her in disgust, as if she'd just said the stupidest thing on earth. 'They're not going to throw *me* out, are they?'

I almost wanted to laugh at this. It was the voice of the old, haughty Pippa – the way she'd been when she'd first come to the Evanova. Luci raised her eyebrows archly. Pippa saw the look. 'Oh –' she said, shaking her head and waggling her hands, 'you know what I mean. Anyway, look–'

'Yes – who are the four people? Tell us,' said Luci obediently.

Pippa held up a hand to count off the four on her fingers.

'One,' she said. 'Alex Brodie. Well – I must say I had my doubts about him when I saw him in the British National Ballet show at Christmas. He's quite good at *grand allegro*, but he can't hold a high extension for toffee, and as for his *batterie*–'

'Two?' said Luci impatiently.

'OK. Two, David Wilder–'

'Oh, not David!' Luci wailed. 'He's about the only boy in our year that's all right–'

'Oh?' said Pippa with a mischievous look. 'I never knew you *liked* him, Luci.'

'Oh, get serious!' Luci rolled her eyes to the ceiling. 'He's just not as obnoxious as Guy Jenkins, that's all. No chance *he's* one of the four, I suppose?'

Pippa shook her head. ''Fraid not. So, three. Mary-Beth Lacey.'

'Not a complete surprise,' said Sadie quietly. 'What with Miss Latimer not letting her start pointe work at the same time as everyone else last term.'

'I bet she cried buckets!' said Pippa with a knowing look. Mary-Beth was the resident cry-baby of our year. She could be relied on to burst into tears at the slightest opportunity. Mind you, I think anyone would have cried at this piece of news.

'And four?' I said.

'Four,' repeated Pippa. 'Rachel Cooper.'

I gasped. 'And not Melanie?'

Pippa looked at me. 'Not, Melanie. Can you imagine it? You're asked to leave and your twin sister isn't!'

'Nightmare!' said Luci. 'Boy, I'm glad I don't have a twin sister!'

'Melanie must feel really bad about it too,' said Sadie.

'Not half as bad as Rachel,' said Pippa.

'So who told you all this?' I asked.

'Miss Lum – just now,' said Pippa. 'She said not to tell anyone – but – well, I could hardly not tell you lot, could I?' She shrugged. 'Anyway, Miss Lum asked me to keep an eye on Mary-Beth and Rachel. You know – see if they were bearing up OK.'

'You?' Luci snorted.

'Yes.' Pippa looked piqued. 'Why? What's wrong with that?'

'Oh nothing,' shrugged Luci. 'I just never saw you as the Florence Nightingale of our year.'

'Anyway, how can you be particularly nice to them without letting on that you know?' said Sadie.

'Oh, everyone'll know soon enough,' said Pippa.

'How come?'

'Well – Miss Lum told Josie Wells too. So – it'll be all over the school in – what?'

'Five minutes?' Sadie offered.

'Less,' said Luci.

There was a pause. Then, 'Wow,' Sadie sighed. 'Just think: wouldn't it be awful to start this term knowing that it was your last.'

Luci nodded. 'They must feel terrible. Can you imagine it?'

It was too much for me. I couldn't hold it in any longer.

'Ella!' Pippa exclaimed, rushing over and taking my hand. 'What's wrong?'

'I – I'm sorry,' I sniffed, swallowing hard to try to stop the tears.

Sadie put her arm round my waist. 'What is it? You can tell us.'

I nodded, but it was another minute before I could speak again.

'My mother's going to have a baby,' I said.

'But that's brilliant!' cried Pippa. 'Lucky you!'

'Is *that* what's wrong?' Sadie was looking at me narrowly.

'I . . .' I stopped. It felt horrible to say it, but I couldn't lie. 'Yes,' I admitted at last. 'Because –' I looked up at the three anxious faces. 'Because it means I'm going to have to leave the Evanova.'

In an instant, anxiety changed to horror. Everyone spoke at once.

'*Leave*?'

'*What*?'

'*No*!'

I looked down at my hands. Without knowing it I'd grabbed fistfuls of the bedspread and was gripping them so hard my knuckles had gone white.

'My mum and dad haven't got enough money for the fees,' I explained. 'It's been difficult for them all year anyhow – but this baby means they definitely can't afford them. Mamma says she'll write to Madame to see if there's a chance of a scholarship, but–'

'But when we auditioned last year they told us there weren't any,' said Sadie.

'Exactly.' I bit my lip. I didn't trust myself to say any more without starting to cry again.

'Look, Ella. There's nothing to worry about,' said Pippa confidently. 'I'll write to Daddy straight away. I'm sure he'll be able to sort it out. Give your parents a loan or something. It's just small change to him–'

'No!' I said hastily. Pippa looked startled. 'I mean – no, thank you. I'm sure . . . that is, I *know* my parents would never want to rely on anyone else's money.'

'But surely, if it meant you could stay here?'

'They wouldn't take it. Trust me. I know,' I said. 'My father is a proud man. He hated Nonna helping to pay for my air fare this Easter – and she is family. I knew he'd never accept money from strangers. Not in a million years.'

'Well,' Sadie looked across at Luci, and then they both turned back to me. 'There's bound to be a scholarship,' she said. But she didn't look certain.

'Sure there is,' Luci added, managing a broader smile. 'Ella – all the teachers love you! They'll never let you leave. You'll see!'

Five

'And so Elizabeth's reign came to an end in 1603.'

Mr Crowther, our history teacher, turned his back on us and began to clean the board. I stared down at the text book in front of me. *Tudors and Stuarts: The Making of Britain*, it was called. It looked like a pretty old copy. The cover was creased and its corners had gone white and furry. Next to me, Pippa – who'd had the job of giving the books out today – had got herself a much newer, smarter one. But I liked my battered old book. It was a bit of history in itself.

I turned to the inside front cover, where the gummed label had been stuck that you were supposed to write your name on. You could tell how old the book was from this; the form was almost filled up with names.

'Felicity Bennett'. The first name was written in large, scrawling capitals. It almost took up the line below it too, making the next name down rather difficult to read. The second name was written in small, careful, joined-up writing: 'Lily Dempsey'.

My eyes widened. *The* Lily Dempsey? The Evanova's most famous ex-pupil? There could hardly have been two, I supposed.

So, Lily Dempsey, now a ballerina who danced with companies all over the world, had once read about the Tudors and the Stuarts from this very book. I ran the flat of my hand over the page. She'd touched this, when she was just a pupil here too, like me.

But not like me, of course, I thought with a sigh. Lily Dempsey had never had to face leaving the school because her parents couldn't pay the fees. Would there ever be a girl sitting here in years to come, looking at *my* name in a book and wishing she could be like the famous ballerina, Gabriella Bruni?

'Someone had to ride to Scotland to take King James VI the news that he'd become James I of England too.'

Mr Crowther was sitting at his desk now, absent-mindedly tickling his cheek with the end of his tie. We had nearly finished this topic. These books would probably be collected up at the end of this lesson and we wouldn't use them again.

I picked up my ink pen and clicked off the cap. Then, in the single remaining spare line at the bottom of the label, I wrote as neatly as I could: 'Gabriella Bruni'. I sat back and looked at it. That proved that I'd been here. Even if I had to leave, my name was there. I'd made my mark.

Pippa nudged me. 'You don't have to do that. We're not keeping them,' she whispered, waving a finger at the label.

I nodded. 'Oh, right.' Then I looked back to Mr Crowther.

Mr Crowther had spotted a hand swaying in the air.

'Yes, Guy?' he said.

Guy Jenkins, the resident loud-mouth of our year, with nail-brush hair and a nose that looked like he'd had a lump of putty thrown at his face, swung back on his chair. I was sure he was going to ask something stupid. He always did. Like, 'What do we do History *for*, Mr Crowther?' That one always got Mr Crowther upset.

Guy cleared his throat. 'How come James was next in line to the throne, Mr Crowther?' he said.

There was a shuffle as everyone turned to look at him. Was this a wind-up? But no – there was a genuine look of puzzlement on his face. He'd asked a serious question!

Mr Crowther looked astonished. 'That,' he said, 'is a very good question, Guy. I wonder if anyone here can answer it?'

Mr Crowther glanced round the room. 'Why *was* it James who inherited the crown?' he repeated hopefully. His eyes rested on me. Don't ask me, I thought, looking away quickly. Not today. Please don't speak to me. Please–

'Ella?' he said.

I studied the top of my desk. 'I – erm . . . Because . . .'

'Oh!' exclaimed Mr Crowther suddenly, tapping a finger towards me in mid-air. 'Ella – yes!' He bounced up from his seat and started to rummage in his briefcase, bringing out files and haphazard piles of paper.

I looked up at him in confusion.

'Message – for you – I'm sure I – wrote down–' mumbled Mr Crowther, becoming more frenzied in his search, flinging his briefcase aside and patting the pockets of his jacket. 'Aha!' he cried at last, pulling out a crumpled piece of paper. 'Here it is!'

The next search was for his reading glasses, which occupied him for a few more minutes, before they turned up in the bottom of the briefcase he'd just been looking through.

'Ye-es . . .' said Mr Crowther, scanning the piece of paper rapidly, then looking up at me again. 'Ella. You are requested to go to Miss Featherstone's office at break.'

'Oh,' I said. 'OK. Thank you.'

'So.' Mr Crowther crushed the paper in his hand and tossed it in the direction of the bin. It missed, but he'd already turned away by that time. 'Where were we?' he said, looking at the blackboard. 'Ah yes! James VI. Can anyone tell me *why*?'

The office belonging to Miss Featherstone, the school secretary, had a little box fixed to the wall outside. There were two lights on it. One was red, with 'Busy – Please wait' written beside it, and then below that there was a green light, with 'Knock and wait' in the same thick black letters. Approaching along the corridor, I could already see that the red light was on. When I drew level with the door, the faint murmur of Miss Featherstone's voice drifted out to me through the thick wood.

I shifted from foot to foot impatiently, staring up at the pictures on the walls, then out of the corridor window to the lawn beyond, and then down the passageway, which faded into darkness. What did she want to see me for? Had the cheque Mamma sent for my new pointe shoes bounced *again*? What excuse could I give this time?

The umpteenth time I turned back to check that the light was still red, I heard the clunk of the telephone receiver going down and, just at that moment, the light flicked to green. I sprang to the door, in case it might change again, and knocked sharply.

'Come in!'

The round brass handle turned easily and I crossed the threshold.

'Wait, child, wait!' Behind her desk, Miss Featherstone shot out one hand like a policewoman directing the traffic, while with the other she noted something down on a clipboard that she had in front of her.

'Monday at eleven,' she said to herself. Then she picked up the clipboard, and hung it on a hook on the wall behind her. Several other clipboards were hanging there in a neat row already. At last she looked across at me.

I was still standing by the door.

'*Yes*. Gabri*ella*,' she said, motioning me towards her. I approached her desk, wondering how she could bear to wear a thick woolly jumper when her radiator was on full blast.

'Your mother wrote a letter to *Madame*, did she not?'

My heart skipped a beat. I didn't know Mamma had done it already. 'Erm. Yes,' I said hesitantly.

'On the subject of *scholarships* . . .'

In what seemed to me like slow motion, Miss Featherstone drew out a piece of paper from a file in front of her. I looked at it as she set it down on the desk. There was something typed on it, but I couldn't decipher it upside down.

'*Well.*' She clasped her hands together and looked at me. 'What? What?' I wanted to scream. I couldn't stand the suspense.

'As we wrote to *all* parents at the beginning of this academic year, our scholarships have been *greatly* reduced by the *unfortunate* loss of one of our benefactors. However –' Miss Featherstone tapped the paper before her. 'There *is* in fact one scholarship that remains available for the funding of a student's *second* year at this school. Providing, that is, it is a case of *genuine* hardship.' Miss Featherstone looked at me over her half-moon spectacles.

I tried desperately to look like a case of genuine hardship. But all I could do was grin. There *was* a scholarship! There *was* hope! I was so happy I could have thrown open Miss Featherstone's window and floated out of it across the lawn like a helium balloon.

'The scholarship is called the Beckwith Medal,' Miss Featherstone went on. 'It will only fund the student for *one* year – if you received it, you would have to make alternative arrangements *thereafter* . . .'

'What do I have to do?' I said quickly. If this Beckwith Medal had bought just one extra month at the Evanova, I would still have done anything to get it.

'You do not have to *do* anything,' said Miss Featherstone. 'Except work very *hard*, of course, as we expect you to do at *all times*. The Scholarship Committee meets just before the end of term. All your teachers will *report* on your progress – your results in this term's *academic* exams will be taken into account as well as your *vocational* work. And your *general* conduct will be considered, too. The Committee will *compare* your reports with those of *other* candidates and *then* make their decision.'

'So – I won't know until the end of term?' I said breathlessly.

'That is correct,' said Miss Featherstone.

'The end of *term*?' Pippa repeated. She dropped the daisy-chain she'd just been making.

I nodded.

'But that's ages away! It's ridiculous! I can't stand the suspense!'

'*You* can't?' Sadie turned to look at her. 'What about Ella?'

'Oh, you poor thing!' Pippa gave me a hug.

We were sitting in our favourite place in the school grounds: the little clearing by the old beech tree. Pippa had brought her winter cape to sit on, but Sadie and I were braving the damp.

I tore up some blades of grass and scattered them on the air. 'I'm not worried about that. I've just had the best bit of news in the world! I don't care how long I have to wait – as long as there's a chance for me – however small.'

'Small?' said a voice behind me. It was Luci. She'd spread out her blazer under the beech tree, and was reclining on it, like a Roman on a couch. 'Ella – you're bound to get this scholarship! There'll be no contest.'

'Is there anyone else going in for it?' asked Pippa.

'I don't know,' I said. 'Miss Featherstone did mention something about other candidates.'

'I bet there aren't any,' said Sadie. 'I bet it's just a ploy to get you to work really hard all term.'

'No change there!' laughed Luci. 'Ella's the hardest worker in our year, I reckon.' She rolled a leaf between her fingers and lobbed it at me. 'You're brilliant at ballet, and you get A's in all your subjects too. Who could compete with that?'

'I'm going to *have* to get A's now,' I said, thinking about it properly for the first time. 'And I'll have to do well in these exams after half-term too.'

'No worries!' Luci grinned at me.

'That's easy for you to say,' I began uncertainly. But Luci didn't want to hear my doubts.

'We'll help!' she cut in. 'Sadie can go over your maths with you, since she's such a whizz at that, you and me can go over our English stuff together and Pippa . . .'

Luci suddenly looked stumped. 'Pippa . . .' she

began again, hoping for inspiration, 'will help you with . . .'

Pippa looked puzzled and then offended as she worked out the reason for Luci's pause. She folded her arms and stared at Luci archly. 'Yes?'

'. . . will help you with . . . whatever you like!' Luci finished.

'I've been working really hard, thank you very much,' said Pippa. 'Well, since the end of last term, anyway.'

'Yeah,' said Luci, with a wicked gleam in her eye, 'which adds up to – what? About three and a half weeks?'

Once upon a time Pippa would have been offended by Luci's teasing, but now she just shrugged and said, 'It's quality not quantity that counts.'

We all laughed at that one.

I flipped down on my back. 'I don't mind about working hard though,' I said, smiling up at the branches above me. 'I'll do whatever it takes. I'd do anything to stay here.'

'You love us all that much!' laughed Luci.

'That's right!'

'Phew – thank goodness we don't have to worry about that any more,' said Pippa, as if everything was settled. 'I couldn't have stood spending the whole term thinking it might be your last, Ella! So – what about this gala they're putting on for Madame, then?'

Six

Pippa was first through the door. She turned round to face the rest of us as we followed her into the studio, and jerked her thumb back at the clock on the wall. 'I told you your watch was fast, Sadie! It's not even half past yet.'

'All the more time for warming up then,' said Luci, flinging her pointe shoes into the corner with a clatter.

'Who cares about warming up?' Pippa leant back against the barre and checked her reflection in the mirror. 'Miss Latimer'll only give us fifty-six *plié* exercises anyhow – you know her!'

'Ah, Pippa – such dedication to your art!' Luci laughed and then turned to look at me. 'Hey, Ella – you all right? You're standing there like a lost sheep.'

I nodded and grinned at Luci. 'Fine.' I placed my pointe shoes carefully in the corner by the rosin box, then took up my place at the barre.

Dempsey Studio was familiar to me now – it was where we'd had all our ballet lessons this year – with Miss Latimer and, last term, with our new teacher Carlos Vasquez, too.

But somehow, this morning, it felt different. I felt like a new girl again, noticing everything afresh – the smell of floor polish and Windowlene; the soft creak of the shiny, sprung boards beneath my feet; the smooth grain of the wooden barre under my fingers, and the sunlight shining down on me from the window above. There were the hefty old radiators, too, with their peeling white paint. In winter they seemed to give out no heat at all, yet they still burnt your legs if you leant against them. The wall opposite was entirely covered with mirrors, making the studio seem twice as big as it really was. And in the far corner, there was the grand piano, with its adjustable stool, where the pianist, Mr Judd, would soon be sitting, staring dolefully at us as always over the lid.

This felt like home. I wanted to breathe it all in – to savour every moment – every sight, sound and smell.

'Don't sit in the bottom of your *pliés,* girls. Constant movement is what I want to see.'

A little less than twenty minutes later, the room had filled with more bodies, all in their school uniform of dark blue leotard and pink tights. Miss Latimer, a vision this morning in lilac chiffon, was walking along the line as we stood at the barre, supervising us as we bent and stretched our legs in time to the music. She paused here and there to adjust a hand, or a head, or to correct the position of a pointed foot.

'Make your arm movements soft – it's a *port de bras*, remember. Good girl, Ella!'

I drank in her praise. I'd always cared desperately what Miss Latimer thought of my work – but suddenly this term, it was more important than ever. She and Carlos would be reporting to the Scholarship

Committee. I had to show her in every single lesson how hard I could work, and just how much I loved my dancing.

The *plié* music drew to a close. Somewhere behind me, I heard a sniff. I glanced in the mirror, but couldn't tell where it was coming from. Someone must have a cold, I thought.

'*Battements tendus.* Watch carefully, girls.' Miss Latimer demonstrated what she wanted. '*Tendu* to the front, to the side, to the back, to the side, then four *tendus* to the side, closing the first one in front: and 5, and 6, and 7, and 8. Then start again to the back.'

I was determined to make each movement better each time I repeated it. Every *tendu*, every *plié* had to be better than the last one, and tomorrow's work would have to be better than today's . . .

As the music struck up and I prepared my arm into second position, I checked my reflection. I wished I had Pippa's long legs, which seemed to go on for ever, and which she could lift much higher than I could lift mine. I wished I had Luci's energy; she made even the slowest movements seem bright – she seemed to shine when she was dancing with a radiance all her own; and I wished I had Sadie's amazing smoothness of movement – she could make the steps run into each other as if they came to her naturally, and weren't an exercise set by the teacher at all.

What did I have? Neat footwork, I knew that; I was always careful to keep my legs turned out; to close my feet exactly in fifth position at the end of a step; to touch my heels to the floor when I landed in between jumps. But I couldn't jump as high as Luci, or as gracefully as Sadie, and though I had good feet that pointed well, I knew my 'line', as Miss Latimer called it, was nowhere near as beautiful as Pippa's.

Sniff, sniff, came the sound from behind me.

'Feel as if you're throwing your foot into the air on a *grand battement* – not that you need a crane to haul it up!' commanded Miss Latimer a couple of exercises later.

'Throwing my foot,' I repeated to myself as I swung my leg up to the front. I wanted to remember everything Miss Latimer said.

Sniff, sniff. There it was again.

Miss Latimer clapped her hands to stop the music.

'Mary-Beth Lacey!' she said sharply. 'You're all over the place this morning! You're swinging back atrociously on your supporting leg.' Miss Latimer stopped and approached Mary-Beth. 'What is it, child?'

So that was where the sniffing had been coming from.

Mary-Beth pulled out a handkerchief that she'd had tucked up in the leg of her leotard, and blew her nose noisily.

'I'm sorry, Miss La–' she began. 'I – I –' But she couldn't go on.

'Pull yourself together, girl!' commanded Miss Latimer testily. 'Are you ill?'

Still crying, Mary-Beth shook her head.

Miss Latimer walked to the front of the studio, and

signalled for Mr Judd to start playing again. But two bars later she changed her mind.

'Oh, for goodness' sake, Mary-Beth!' she snapped. 'If you can't stop snivelling, get out of my class!'

Mary-Beth didn't wait to be told again. She headed for the door.

Miss Latimer adjusted her chiffon scarf and cleared her throat. 'Now – let's come into the centre, girls, shall we?'

Last term, when Miss Latimer or Carlos had been working us particularly hard, I'd often longed for the hands on the studio clock to speed up, and for class to be over, so I could rest my aching legs and feet. Now, though, I wanted to eek out every minute I had, and when Miss Latimer finally called for Mr Judd to play the music for our curtsies, I felt disappointed it was over so soon.

'And – rest,' said Miss Latimer when we'd finished. 'Stand at ease for a moment, girls. There is something I wish to talk to you about.

'I expect that you have all by now heard about the gala performance we are to give in honour of Madame's eightieth birthday at the end of this term.'

Murmurs of 'yes' circulated round the class.

'Each year in the school,' said Miss Latimer, 'is to perform separately. Mr Edwards, Mr Vasquez and I have decided that the First Year will perform a new piece – to be choreographed by me – ' a self-satisfied smile crept on to Miss Latimer's face – 'to the famous piece of Tchaikovsky music: "The Waltz of the

Flowers". You will be working in partnership with the boys' – a faint groan could be heard. Miss Latimer ignored it – 'which will be excellent early practice for you in some of the basic techniques of *pas de deux*. Everyone in the year will take part in this piece, and there will also be a leading couple who will perform a short *pas de deux* on their own.'

There was a rustle of shifting feet around the room as every girl entertained the brief hope that the couple would include her.

'After consultation with Mr Edwards and Mr Vasquez,' said Miss Latimer, 'we have chosen Guy Jenkins and –' She paused briefly, enjoying the suspense. I looked at Pippa. It would be her, I was certain. Everyone knew she was Miss Latimer's favourite pupil. 'Gabriella Bruni!' announced Miss Latimer.

Pippa's face fell momentarily. Then, the next instant, she turned to me with a generous smile. At my other side, Sadie patted my arm. In the mirror, I saw Luci cross her eyes at me and mouth 'Guy!' with a grimace.

I laughed. I felt buffeted by the congratulations. I looked at Miss Latimer – she was smiling at me softly, and gave me a small nod. Was it true? She'd chosen me – out of the whole class?

'Rehearsals will start the week after next,' Miss Latimer went on. 'They will take place in the afternoons, after school lessons. Needless to say, you will be expected to carry on doing your homework just as usual – the academic staff will not take these rehearsals as an excuse for laziness. I know you have very important academic exams just after half-term.'

When we were finally allowed to go, I dashed for my shoes and, without waiting for the others as I usually did, I sprinted down the corridor towards the changing rooms. I hadn't forgotten about Mary-Beth. I hoped she might still be there.

Sure enough, when I got down the stairs into the changing room, I saw a lonely figure slumped on the bench, already changed into her school clothes, with her bag slung over her shoulder, and her head bowed. She was still sniffing, gently.

'Mary-Beth?' I stopped in front of her, clutching my pointe shoes to my chest.

She looked up, her eyes puffy and red, and her cheeks blotchy. She rubbed her nose with her handkerchief. 'Yes?'

Suddenly I didn't know quite what to say. I shrugged. 'I just wanted to see if you were all right.'

Mary-Beth sniffed again. 'Who cares?'

'I do.' I sat on the bench. She didn't move her bag to make way for me so it stayed between us.

'Is – is it about having to leave?' I ventured.

Mary-Beth didn't look at me. But she nodded.

'I thought it might be.' I looked down at my pointe shoes, winding and unwinding the ribbons as I talked. 'I just wanted to say – I know what you're going through.'

Mary-Beth shook her head energetically. 'No, you

don't!' she said, looking at me blearily. 'How could you?'

I gripped my shoes tighter. I hadn't wanted anyone else in the year to know, but perhaps it would help. 'I might have to leave too,' I said. 'My mum and dad can't afford the fees for next year.'

Mary-Beth turned her head sharply and searched my face for any sign that I was kidding. 'Really?'

I nodded. 'The thing is–'

But I didn't get any further. The next moment, Luci clattered down the steps two at a time and, grabbing my hands, dragged me to my feet and whirled me round.

'Congrats, Ella! You're a star! And it's all the proof you need – you'll definitely get it now!'

'Get what?' said Mary-Beth behind me.

Before I could stop her, Luci blurted, 'The Beckwith Medal. It's a scholarship Ella's going in for to help with her fees.' As Mary-Beth's face clouded over, Luci turned back to me. 'But now you've got the main part in the show, they could hardly not keep you on, could they?'

'A scholarship!' snapped Mary-Beth, tears welling up in her eyes again. 'So you're not going to have to leave at all! What was that little speech for, then? You were just laughing at me, weren't you?' She stood up.

'Mary-Beth–' I began, reaching for her arm.

But she side-stepped me. 'You *don't* know how I feel,' she said. 'You don't! But I wish you did!'

And with that, she stumped up the changing-room

steps, barging past the people coming down.

Luci looked after her, stunned, for a moment, then turned back to me. 'Did I say something wrong?'

I shook my head. 'Never mind. I just made a mess of something. I thought perhaps I could make Mary-Beth feel a bit better. But I doubt that anyone can just now. And you can't really blame her, can you?'

'I don't see why she has to take it out on us,' said Pippa, frowning. 'I mean, the teachers have done her a favour, really. If she's not good enough to make it as a dancer, it's better to know sooner rather than later.'

I caught sight of Rachel Cooper, then, giving Pippa a hard stare across the changing room. Pippa flushed pink and said no more.

Seven

'One performance, is that all it is?'

Melanie Cooper nodded. 'I reckon it's because the Grand Theatre must be really expensive to hire out.'

'Seems an awful lot of work to do for just one performance!' said Josie Wells wearily.

'It is in honour of our beloved Madame's birthday,' Luci reminded her, with mock reverence.

'But – straight after our school exams! I mean, it's all very well Miss Latimer saying we'll have to get all our homework done as well as this rehearsing, but there are only so many hours in a day! What does she expect? That we'll do our homework in our sleep?'

'Moan, moan, moan!' laughed Luci. 'It's a chance to perform at the Grand, right? We don't get that too often!'

'And I'm glad they're letting Mary-Beth and the others who are leaving have parts in it,' I said, glancing across to where Mary-Beth and Rachel Cooper were sitting together. I still felt guilty about my disastrous conversation with Mary-Beth. 'Otherwise there really would be no point to this term for them at all.'

Luci wafted her spoon in the air. 'I shall choreograph a masterpiece to the tune of "Waltz of the Flowers",' she declared, doing a remarkably good impression of Miss Latimer.

The rest of us at the dining table giggled.

'Isn't it just typical Miss Latimer!' said Luci, using her own voice again.

'What?'

'Finding a piece of music called "Waltz of the *Flowers*". I'm surprised it's not "Waltz of the Fairies" or something.' Luci held one hand up before her. 'I can see it now – we'll have flowers in our hair, and drift around the stage in floaty dresses – and you lot'll look wonderful, and I'll look a complete pudding!' She laughed. 'Why couldn't she cast me as the gardener or something?'

Sadie glanced up to the teacher's table at the top of the hall. I followed her gaze. A dark-haired man with a proud profile had just sat down there to tuck into his meal. Sadie nodded towards him. 'I bet you wish it was Carlos doing the choreography instead, don't you Luci?'

'Too right, I do!' Luci leant back in her seat to look at him. Then she turned to us and grinned. 'What'd it be, d'you reckon? Something Spanish?' She snatched Josie's spoon out of her bowl, rattling it against her own like castanets, and stamping her feet under the table. 'Olé!'

'Shhh! He'll hear you!' giggled Sadie.

'Have you quite finished?' asked Josie sarcastically, holding out her hand for her spoon. Luci spun it back to her down the table.

'Well, dream on,' said Pippa. 'It looks like Carlos is steering well clear of the whole thing.'

'No, hang on.' Luci leant forward, with an eager expression. 'Never mind Carlos. I tell you what I really wish.' She tapped the table with her finger. 'I wish I was choreographing something for the show myself.'

'*You*?' Pippa raised her eyebrows in disbelief.

'Why not? I ended up making up half of that dance in the Christmas show, remember? And Robin Bell said it was good.'

Robin Bell was the choreographer at the British National Ballet. He'd choreographed the show we'd been in at Christmas.

'If I want to be a choreographer one day . . .' said Luci.

'In between running your own company and all those other things you're going to do,' I put in.

'Of course. Well, if I do want to be one, I ought to get the practice in now. And – hey!' added Luci, visibly warming to the idea. 'This birthday gala is supposed to be showing off the work of the school and the abilities of the students, right?'

'Well – yes, I suppose that's true,' said Sadie.

'So they *should* let me do some choreography. They'd be wrong not to!' Luci scraped back her chair and stood up.

'Where are you going?' Sadie asked anxiously. 'I haven't finished my baked apple yet.'

'Just going to have a word with Carlos,' said Luci. 'Back in a sec!'

Still not quite believing it, we watched her march off to the far end of the hall.

'The cheek of it!' said Pippa, shaking her head. 'Going up to a teacher like that with her mad ideas!'

'I bet he'll say yes,' I said, looking up towards the top table. I could see Carlos talking animatedly to Luci. He didn't look at all angry.

'I bet he will too!' said Sadie excitedly. 'He likes Luci.'

Pippa nodded knowingly and tapped the side of her head. 'They're *both* mad.'

The next moment, we saw Luci wending her way back to our table, getting curious looks from other pupils, who'd seen her talking to Carlos, as she passed.

'Well!' she plumped down in her seat again. 'Carlos says he doesn't see why there shouldn't be one extra piece added to the programme – as long as it's short, of course. In fact, he thinks it's a great idea! He's going to propose it at the next staff meeting.'

'So it's not *definite* then?' said Pippa.

'Not absolutely. But – come on!' Luci looked round at us with a grin. 'Can you imagine Carlos not getting his way when he's decided on something?'

Sadie laughed. 'Not likely!'

Luci rubbed her hands together. 'Right! I think we should start work on it straight away!'

'We?'

'The four of us!' said Luci. 'You're all in it of course.' She laughed. 'I have just cast my first ballet!'

Pippa looked doubtful. 'I'm not sure I–'

'Pippa,' said Luci. 'Listen. It's a chance to be in two things in the gala instead of just one.'

'That's true,' said Pippa, considering it, her head on one side.

I leant forward across the table. 'Luci. I'd love to be in it – really I would. But I've got that *pas de deux* with Guy – that'll mean extra rehearsals on top of the ones the whole class has together. And I'll need to do so much work for these school exams–'

'Aw, come on Ella –' Luci looked at me pleadingly. 'I can't leave you out!'

'It's a chance for the four of us to dance together!' said Sadie.

'My first chance to choreograph something!' added Luci. 'Surely – you won't let me down?'

'OK, OK!' I laughed. 'I'd love to do it.'

'That's more like it!' Luci grinned. 'This is going to be fantastic. I just know it!'

Eight

'I wish I knew dance notation.' Luci pulled a curl of hair round to her mouth and chewed on it. 'Trying to write down steps in normal words takes forever. You cover half a page just describing one movement.'

'I think we'll be starting on notation classes next year,' said Sadie, looking up from her book.

Next year. The words touched off a shiver of worry in my head.

'Which sort of notation do they teach here?' I asked.

'There's more than one?' Sadie looked surprised.

'Oh, yes,' said Pippa. 'There's Benesh notation and Labanotation.'

'One's sort of dots and squiggles put on those sets of five lines they use for music, isn't it?' offered Luci.

'They're called staves,' put in Sadie.

'That's Benesh notation,' said Pippa. 'And then Labanotation –'

'OK, OK,' Luci interrupted. 'It's not much use to me now, is it?'

It was a wet lunchtime, and we'd gone to the library to do some work. Well, I'd said I was going and the others said they'd come with me. 'For support,' Luci had said.

Which was nice of them. Except that, since none of them – unlike me – had started on their revision for the exams yet, they weren't exactly the best company if you wanted to get a lot of work done.

'Eliz I reigned 1558–1603,' I wrote. I was making notes on sheets of paper from all the work we'd done this year. I condensed it into note form, then tried to learn from that.

Pippa stretched back and scanned the bookcase just to her left. 'Oh, look,' she said, pulling on one of the spines. 'It's a book about Mummy!'

'Let's see,' said Sadie.

'1558,' I repeated to myself, hoping it would go in. '1603–'

'Hey, here's a picture of Carlos!'

I looked up, exasperated.

'Sorry, Ella,' said Sadie. 'We disturbing you?'

'Yes, shhh, guys,' said Luci sternly. 'Nothing's as important as Ella's work, right?'

The others nodded, and solemnly read their books in silence.

It lasted about thirty seconds. Then Luci herself, who had been staring across to the other side of the library, leant forward and said,

'You know, something's been bothering me.'

Sadie looked up. 'What?'

Luci nodded her head in the direction of the far table. 'Guy Jenkins. What's up with him this term?'

'What do you mean?'

'Well –just look at him.' We all did. There, with his work spread out over half the table, Guy Jenkins, who'd never been known to open a book willingly before in his life, was working diligently.

'Wow!' said Sadie. 'I don't think I've ever seen him in the library on a wet break before. Usually, he just hangs around the cloakrooms with Alex or Vaz, having spitting competitions.'

'Or sticking chewing gum to people's blazers,' added Pippa with distaste.

'Yes, I know. But have you noticed him in lessons this term?' said Luci. 'He's so – so quiet. No throwing bits of chewed up paper or flicking ink at people's backs.'

'Perhaps he's seen the light,' giggled Sadie. 'He's a changed person.'

Suddenly, I had a disturbing idea. I could only think of one reason that would make someone like Guy start working hard. 'Oh no.'

'What? What is it?'

I hardly dared say it. I took a deep breath. 'He could be going for the Beckwith Medal, too.'

'No way!' said Sadie. 'Why would he be doing that?'

I shrugged. 'Same reason as me, I would have thought.'

Luci looked troubled.

'It makes sense, doesn't it?' I said.

'It *would* explain it. But I'm sure there's some other reason,' said Pippa firmly.

'I have to know,' said Luci. 'Right now.' She scraped her chair back and got up.

'You're not going to ask him?' Sadie looked up at her in shock.

'Nah, silly.' Luci shook her head. 'I'll ask David.'

David Wilder was sitting a table away from Guy. Luci hurried over to him, and leaned on her tummy over the table. I saw David jut his head forward to catch what she was saying. Then he glanced briefly at Guy before he replied.

Luci rushed back. 'Ella,' she said, sliding into her seat again and looking at me. 'You're right. David heard Alex and Guy talking about it this morning.'

I sat perfectly still, holding my breath. I hadn't realised how used I'd got to the idea that I was the only candidate for the Beckwith Medal – until that moment.

Sadie shook me gently.

'Come on – you aren't worried, are you?' she said.

'Yeah,' Luci snorted. 'If that's your only competition, Ella, you can relax. It's in the bag.'

'The idea of Guy Jenkins getting it!' Pippa laughed heartily.

'Is he any good?' I asked. 'At dancing I mean.'

'Any good?' Luci frowned, considering. 'I haven't seen him dance since the show at Christmas . . . Jeepers, it's hard to remember. He was OK.'

'They've chosen him for this *pas de deux* –' I pointed out.

'True,' said Luci.

'They've chosen you too, don't forget!' Sadie slapped me on the shoulder.

'Anyway, you told us they take everything into account for this scholarship,' said Luci. 'Your schoolwork, your behaviour. The teachers hate him!'

'Yes, but if he's trying hard this term,' I said, nodding over towards him again. The others turned to look. 'The teachers'll probably be more pleased with him because he's never worked before.'

'The lost sheep returns to the fold,' said Sadie.

'Nightmare!' muttered Luci, watching Guy. Then she put her hand out and took mine comfortingly. 'No worries, Ella. I still don't reckon he stands a chance against you. I mean – you've been working like a Trojan all year. He can't possibly make up for that in one term! And all the teachers know how nice you are. Responsible–'

Sadie nodded. 'Trustworthy–'

'What's that word they put on reports? Conscientious–'

'Mature–'

'Stop, stop!' I laughed. 'Too much!'

A few minutes later, when Luci had gone back to her choreography notes, and Sadie and Pippa were reading the book about Pippa's mother again, I was just staring at the paper in front of me, letting the words swim before my eyes. Thinking.

I'd never felt especially competitive about anything before. I'd always wanted to do my best – but I'd not cared about beating anyone in particular. Now, suddenly, I felt a wave of determination rising up in me. However hard Guy worked, I would work harder. However well he danced, I would have to dance better.

I glanced across at him. As if he felt my gaze, he

looked up. For a fleeting moment, he looked surprised. Then his face hardened, and he stared back at me challengingly.

So, he knew about me, too. Were there others? Or was it just us – one against one? One of us would be able to stay at the school, and one of us would have to leave . . . That was a real contest – and one we were both desperate to win.

'Oh no!' I said suddenly, holding my head. 'I forgot!'

'What?' Luci looked at me.

'The *pas de deux*! Guy and I are going to have to dance together – just the two of us!'

'Weird,' said Sadie. 'I wonder if the teachers chose you before they knew?'

'Must have done,' said Pippa.

Luci grimaced. 'If they did it on purpose, it's a pretty nasty test!'

That was certainly true. And, coincidence or not, I wasn't looking forward to dancing with Guy.

Part Three

A Testing Time

Nine

'You've brought your pointe shoes with you, Ella?' asked Miss Latimer with a friendly smile as she came into the studio.

I nodded.

'Good girl. Put them on straight away then, please.' She set down her bag and picked out of it a small tape recorder, with a long lead which she plugged into the wall-socket.

'I'm afraid we'll have to work from taped music in these extra rehearsals we have together,' she said, 'as Mr Judd is needed for Mrs Seymour's senior class in Tyrrel Studio.'

Quickly, I sat down and began to untie the ribbons on my soft shoes to exchange them for my blocked ones.

Behind me, I heard the studio door swing open.

'Ah, here you are Guy!' said Miss Latimer, looking up. 'You really must try to be absolutely punctual for these rehearsals. We don't have a minute to spare.'

I turned round to see Guy standing behind me, neatly dressed in his white T-shirt and black leggings.

'Yes, Miss Latimer. Sorry, Miss Latimer,' he said politely.

He glanced down at me. Quickly, I looked back to my ribbons.

A few minutes later, Miss Latimer clicked off the tape recorder. 'Lovely music, isn't it?'

I nodded. It was true, 'The Waltz of the Flowers' was beautiful, with a lilting quality that just made you want to dance, even when you didn't know what steps to do!

'Now,' Miss Latimer rewound the tape and listened to the beginning of the music again, her eyes closed. Then she drew in a deep breath and clicked off the tape recorder.

'You will each enter from different sides of the stage. Ella,' she waved me over to one side of the studio. 'Let us have a *bourrée* to begin with, shall we? A beautiful, smooth, floating *bourrée*, from the back corner down to the centre here.' Miss Latimer demonstrated, skimming over the floor with tiny steps, her arms moving as slowly and smoothly as her legs moved rapidly.

I struggled to copy her. Although my pointe work was improving, we'd only been allowed up on pointe for the first time at the end of last term, and I was far from expert. My steps felt awkward, ungainly, compared to Miss Latimer's.

I caught sight of Guy with a smug smile on his

face. Right! I thought. I'll show him!

'Smaller, quicker steps!' commanded Miss Latimer, watching my attempt. 'Here.' She held out her hands for me to hold for balance while I tried again.

'Better!' she said. 'Good girl, Ella!'

I glanced over at Guy. He wasn't smiling now.

When it was Guy's turn to dance, though, I had to admit that he was very good. He could jump well – or, as Miss Latimer would have said, he had 'good *ballon*'.

We did some small supported jumps – nothing dramatic like you see grown-up dancers doing – but still, I could feel that his arms were pretty strong. And his double *pirouette* was rock steady and as clean as a whistle.

Moreover, when Miss Latimer corrected him for something, he didn't make the same mistake again. He was a quick learner.

Steadily, my heart was sinking into my boots. Where was the annoying, wise-cracking loud-mouth, who'd goofed around in all my school lessons for the last two terms? I could have coped with him.

But this was certainly going to be no walk-over. With Guy's dancing this good, I was going to have to do really well in the school exams to be sure of beating him. I made a mental note to do extra revision tonight.

'Step further to the right, or I can't turn you under my arm properly,' Guy said the next minute, as we repeated a particularly tricky sequence.

'Oh – OK.'

'Look at each other! Look at each other!' Miss

Latimer called out from the front of the studio. 'And smile! That's better!'

As Guy and I grimaced at one another obediently, I wondered for the millionth time why they were making us dance together. But Miss Latimer wasn't giving anything away. She never mentioned the scholarship once.

'You've both worked hard today,' she said approvingly when the rehearsal time was up. 'But you must learn to work together more – to help each other. That's the essence of *pas de deux* work. If you don't work together, you both look bad. Remember that.'

Guy and I nodded, but avoided each other's gaze.

'We shall have to measure you for your costumes soon,' said Miss Latimer as she unplugged the tape recorder and wound the flex neatly around her hand.

I glanced up, hoping she would say more.

Miss Latimer was frowning in thought. 'Pale blue for you, Ella, I think,' she said. 'It will go well with your colouring. Yes – a pale blue tutu – then you can wear your normal pink tights and pink shoes . . .'

A tutu? I couldn't conceal my delight. A broad smile spread across my face. I'd never had a chance to wear a tutu before. I would feel like a real ballerina!

'And blue jacket and breeches for you, Guy.'

'What costumes will we wear?' asked Sadie in a muffled voice. Luci had told her to start off curled in a ball on the floor. This meant that when she spoke, it was directly into her knees.

'Don't move!' commanded Luci severely, jumping down from the assembly hall stage, where she'd climbed to try and see – she said – what we'd look like to the audience sitting in the circle. It seemed ridiculous, rehearsing in such a big space – the four of us were rattling around like four peas in an outsize maraca. But Luci had said it was the only room that was free.

'I didn't move!' came the muffled voice again. 'I was only asking–'

'I doubt the school will spend money on making special costumes just for *this*,' said Pippa, who was standing twisted to one side, with her arms reaching upwards.

'What do you mean, "just for this"? Don't let your arms flop!' said Luci.

Pippa sighed, and plonked her arms back where Luci had positioned them.

'Well, it's not exactly a proper bit of the show,' Pippa said to the ceiling.

'It is too!' Luci protested. 'Ella – can you move into the position I'm going to be in – you know, down by Sadie – so I can see what that looks like too?'

I got up off the floor and walked over to Sadie. 'Like this?' I stood above her, with my arms bent squarely up in front of me.

'Spot on!' Luci called.

Pippa still hadn't given up. 'We don't even know it's definitely going to be included in the gala yet.'

'They said yes at the staff meeting, didn't they?' Sadie raised her head.

'Only if we show it to Carlos first to make sure it's good enough.'

'Well, it will be!' Luci stumped up to us. 'If you work hard now, that is. Right – next I'd like–'

Then she glanced at the clock. 'Jeepers! It's half-past five already! And I've still only worked out the opening positions!'

Pippa sighed loudly. 'Tell us about it.'

'No – I think the four *jetés* would look much better this way,' Pippa said, ten minutes after Luci had finally got started on choreographing some steps. Pippa demonstrated what she meant.

'I bet Kenneth Macmillan never had to put up with this,' muttered Luci, her hands on her hips. Then she said out loud: 'Look. Pippa. Who's choreographing this?'

Pippa stopped and turned. 'You are,' she admitted.

'Well, then.' Luci spread her hands. 'If I was Robin Bell of the British National Ballet, would you be telling me you think the steps look better your way? Huh? No – so–'

'But–' Pippa tried again.

'And if you're right and the way I want it isn't very good, I'm going to get the criticism, not you!'

'In that case,' said Pippa, with a shrug, 'you can have it your own way. But don't say I didn't warn you!'

'Yeah, yeah. No worries,' said Luci, as she went back to the tape recorder.

'Pyjamas,' said Sadie suddenly.

Everyone looked at her. 'What?'

'Pyjamas. Well – you said it's called "Dreamers", right? So why not wear pyjamas for the costumes?'

Pippa snorted. 'Don't be ridiculous! Miss Latimer would have a fit! Not to mention Madame when she saw it!'

'I think it's a brilliant idea!' exclaimed Luci. 'Thanks, Sadie! Now,' she pushed the button on the tape recorder, 'from the same place again, OK?'

Ten

On the Saturday that began half-term we all lined up as usual by the school's front door. Pippa and Luci were picked up first, leaving Sadie and me standing in the hallway with our bags.

'That's Mamma there – with Lorenzo.' I pulled the photo out from the folded letter and handed it to Sadie.

'He's the brother who picked you up at the end of last term?' Sadie asked.

I nodded. 'That's right.'

'I remember him,' said Sadie. 'Wow! You can really see your mum's pregnant now. How long till the baby's due?'

'Um –' I counted up. 'Another three and a half months.'

Sadie grinned at me as she handed the photo back. 'It's so exciting! What do you want – a brother or sister?'

With surprise, I realised I hadn't really thought about it. 'A sister, I think,' I said at last. 'I've got enough brothers already. I don't want *another* ganging up on me!'

The school door opened, and Sadie looked over, but it wasn't her mum and dad.

'What does your mum say in the letter, then?' she

asked. 'Is she still feeling sick and stuff? When my mum was having the twins, she was sick in the morning for practically the whole nine months.'

'No, that's all stopped now,' I said. 'But she says she's got a real thing about grapefruit juice and baked beans. They're all she wants – for breakfast, lunch and dinner.'

'Bleugh!' Sadie made a face.

'And the funniest thing is – Mamma's always hated baked beans. Usually she can't eat them to save her life!'

Sadie laughed. Then she looked at me and said, 'Bet you're sad not to be going home today?'

I squeezed her hand. 'Nope,' I said. 'I know how much the train to Edinburgh costs. If I was going home, *that'd* worry me the whole time. Anyhow, I love going to your house. Your parents are really great–'

'And talk of the devil!' Sadie interrupted. 'Here they are!'

I looked over to the doorway. Dr and Mrs Marsh had just that minute walked in. Sadie flew to give them a hug. I stayed back by the cases.

'Hi there, Ella.' Setting Sadie down again, Dr Marsh came over to me and, putting an arm round my shoulders, gave me a sideways hug. 'How are you doing?'

'Fine thanks, Dr Marsh,' I said.

'Simon,' he corrected me. 'Remember?'

'Oh, yes.' I nodded. I'd spent half-term with the Marshes last term too, and I'd spent the whole time trying to get used to calling Sadie's parents by their first names. It felt really odd.

'Where are Thomas and Oliver?' asked Sadie, when we were settled in the car and Mrs Marsh – Jill – was starting up the engine. Thomas and Oliver were Sadie's little twin brothers.

'Tina's looking after them,' Jill said, as she backed out of the parking space and swung the car round towards the entrance archway. 'They're both a bit under the weather, so we thought it'd be better not to bring them.'

'So, Ella,' Simon turned in his seat and looked at us. 'Sadie tells us you're going for a scholarship? That right?'

I glanced at Sadie in surprise. She looked at me sheepishly, then concentrated on untwisting her seat belt.

'Um – yes,' I said.

'And you're bound to get it, as you're a wonderful dancer and work really hard in all your school subjects too!' Simon looked at me with mischief in his eyes.

'Well – ' I frowned. 'I wouldn't –'

Simon laughed. 'I'm sure it's true! As it happens, we were really worried about the school fees when Sadie first applied. In fact, it was touch and go whether you could come here at all, wasn't it, Tiger?'

Tiger was his special name for Sadie. Sadie seemed a bit embarrassed that he used it in front of me.

'Did you know, Ella,' Simon hooked his arm back over the seat so that he could lean towards me conspiratorially, 'that the money for Sadie's school fees this year came from *The Golden Ticket*?' He beamed at me proudly.

'*The Golden Ticket*?' I repeated.

Jill gave a long-suffering sigh. 'It's a television quiz show, Ella,' she said glancing at me in the rear-view mirror. 'I expect you've got better taste than to watch that sort of thing, unlike Simon here.'

'Dad went on it and won,' Sadie explained.

'We'd never have been able to afford the fees otherwise,' said Simon. 'Enough for one holiday and one year at the Evanova, that's what I won. A tidy sum, I can tell you!'

'So –' I glanced at Sadie, wondering whether I should mention what I was thinking. Sadie looked back at me expectantly. 'So –' I said again, 'next year?'

Sadie wasn't in the same situation as me, was she? She'd never mentioned it – and she hadn't applied for the scholarship.

'Will you go on *The Golden Ticket* again, Dr – er, Simon?' I asked.

'Well–'

'The answer's no,' Sadie's mum cut in with a smile. 'Next year the twins will be old enough to start at playgroup, so I'll be able to get a job. We should just about be able to manage – if we tighten our belts.'

'Urgh!' Simon pulled his seat belt up to his throat and crossed his eyes horribly. Sadie and I both giggled.

Later that day, when we were all sitting at the kitchen

table eating dinner, the conversation turned to our plans for the week's holiday.

'It's reading week at the university this week,' said Simon, his sleeve dragging in his plate of casserole as he leant across for the potatoes.

'What's that?'

Simon grinned. 'Sort of like a half-term – so it means my days are freer than usual. Time for some fun!'

'Let's go somewhere!' said Sadie.

'Exactly what I was thinking! And how about Emmerstone Park for starters? We could go tomorrow!'

'Yeah! Excellent!' Sadie clapped her hands. 'It's this place with fun fair rides and a massive adventure playground,' she said, turning to me. 'It's ace!'

'That all right with you, Ella?' asked Simon.

'Uh –' I felt rather awkward about saying this. 'It sounds really great, but – I think I'd better work. I've got stacks of revision I need to do.'

Sadie tugged at my sleeve. 'Oh, come on, Ella. Just one day won't hurt. You're making me feel guilty. It's only the first proper day of half-term tomorrow.'

'Yes, and the exams start the day after we get back.' I reminded her. 'Sorry. Really. I think I'd better.'

'Well of course, Ella. That's fine, if it's what you want,' said Sadie's mum firmly.

'Wow.' Simon raised his eyebrows. 'Talk about dedication. You certainly deserve this scholarship, Ella, that's for sure.'

Eleven

'She worked the whole time!' Sadie declared, the night we got back to school. We were in the dining hall, having supper.

Luci sucked in the end of her long piece of spaghetti with a 'pock!' and grinned at me. 'Did you, Ella?'

'Not really–'

'She did! My mum and dad couldn't believe it. To tell you the truth, I wish I had too. History and Music exams *tomorrow* – I can't believe it's gone so fast.'

'And then a rehearsal after school,' Pippa reminded her. 'I bet Miss Latimer'll have a fit if anyone's forgotten any of their steps over half-term.'

'And *then* a rehearsal for my ballet after that,' added Luci.

'Oh no!' said Pippa and Sadie together.

Luci sighed. 'Look, guys. We've got to show "Dreamers" to Carlos on Wednesday, right? We've hardly any time left and that middle section is still a shambles.'

'But on Tuesday we've got English and Science!' protested Pippa. 'I haven't even looked at either of them yet!'

'And whose fault is that?' said Luci archly. 'If we don't do well on Wednesday, they won't let us be in the show and all the work we've done will be wasted!'

Pippa sighed flamboyantly.

Just then Guy pushed past our table on his way to the kitchens. My three friends fell silent.

'In a funny way, it's sort of helped having him to compete against,' I said, watching him go. 'I mean – without it I wouldn't have known how well I had to do in these exams to be good enough; now I know I have to beat Guy.'

'You don't necessarily have to beat him. School work's just one part of it, remember,' said Luci.

'Yes, but he's a good dancer, right? Maybe I'm as good as him–'

'Maybe? Definitely.'

'Whatever. But if we're neck and neck on the dancing, the exam results might decide it.'

Luci shrugged. 'I've never thought of it that way.'

'Anyway,' Sadie turned to me. 'How are you feeling about the exams tomorrow, Ella?'

I thought about it. Then I nodded. 'All right. I'm fine – cross fingers! – for the Music, and I've just got one more History topic to go over again tonight. Elizabeth the First.'

'Just that? Lucky you!' Luci laughed. 'I'm going to be up all night with my torch under the blankets, I reckon.'

As it turned out, I couldn't make such short work of my one remaining history project as I'd planned.

While Pippa settled down in bed with her whole history file to look through, I turned to the place where my two pages of condensed notes should have been.

'They've gone!'

Pippa looked up. 'What have?'

'My notes,' I said desperately. 'My Elizabeth the First notes. Two pages. Where on earth can they–' I rummaged through the pile of paper again. I couldn't believe it.

'They can't have disappeared. They'll be around somewhere,' said Pippa, getting out of bed and looking around the room vaguely.

'Where then?' I was close to panicking now.

'Well – when did you last see them?'

I thought about it. 'I can't remember. I'm sure I had them . . . The library! The last time I saw them was in the library just before half-term. You know – that day when you and Sadie were going over that Maths stuff together and Luci was moaning about French irregular verbs.'

'Perhaps you dropped them there.'

'I've got to go and find them!' I reached for my blazer and pulled it on over my pyjamas.

Pippa looked aghast. 'You can't do that! It'll be all dark down there. We're not supposed to–'

'I don't care! The exam's first thing after ballet tomorrow. I'll have no time in the morning – I have to have those notes tonight!'

'All well, guys?' Luci, toothbrush in hand, on her way back from the washrooms, poked her head round the door. She looked pretty surprised to see me with my blazer on over my pyjamas, and my bare feet stuffed into my brown school lace-ups.

'What's up, Ella? Doing a midnight flit?'

I just wasn't in the mood for jokes. This felt like a matter of life and death.

'I'm going down to the library,' I said grimly.

'She's lost some of her history notes,' explained Pippa. 'She last saw them in the library –'

'So I'm going there now,' I said, moving for the door.

Luci grabbed my arm as I passed her. 'They lock the library at night, Ella.'

I looked at her. 'Are you serious? Oh, no!'

'Hey, hey!' Luci shook me gently. 'Don't panic, OK? If you're in a stew all night tonight you won't sleep a wink – and then the History exam's not going to go well whether you know your stuff or not, is it?'

I took a deep breath. 'You're right. It's just–'

'I know,' said Luci. 'These exams mean an awful lot to you. We're all rooting for you, too. But, don't freak out. Look – we three can all lend you *our* notes, can't we?'

'But I haven't got time,' I said, looking at my watch. There wasn't long till lights out. 'I just wanted to look at my quick reminder notes.'

Luci smiled gently. 'Better than nothing, huh?'

I managed a smile in return. 'Loads better,' I said. 'Thanks.'

'No sweat.' Luci went back to the door. 'I'll just get my notes and Sadie's. You look out yours too, Pippa.' And she was gone.

* * *

'I can see them.' Luci stood on tiptoe to look through the glass panel near the top of the door. 'Those awful rows of single desks, one behind another. They give me the shivers.'

'I hate it when the teacher comes along and puts the question paper face down in front of you,' said Pippa.

'And there's this horrid jittery quiet, as people fiddle with their pens and pencils,' added Sadie.

'Don't, don't!' I said. 'You're making it worse! I feel bad enough as it is!'

'Did you get through the Elizabeth the First notes OK?' Luci turned away from the door to look at me.

I nodded. 'I think so.'

We lapsed into silence. Behind us, someone laughed. I turned. It was Rachel Cooper. She was whispering with Mary-Beth. They both looked relaxed and not nervous at all.

'Mary-Beth seems to be feeling better these days,' whispered Luci in my ear, seeing which way I was looking. 'I guess it's the one advantage of being asked to leave: it doesn't matter how you do in these exams.'

'Right, people,' said Mr Bronan, coming out of the hall and clapping his hands. 'I hope you've all looked at the desk plan. I don't want anyone wandering around like a lost sheep when they get in there.'

I craned my neck to look round Luci at the plan again. I was in the second column of desks, behind Melanie Cooper and in front of Mary-Beth. Easy enough to remember.

Then the doors opened and we all filed in.

'The time,' said Mr Bronan when we had settled down, 'is exactly 10:05. You have one hour. Remember to write your name on each piece of paper. If you need more paper, put up your hand, but don't shout out. Right – you may begin.'

There was a fluttering sound all over the hall as nervous fingers turned over exam papers.

What felt like about ten minutes later, Mr Bronan looked at his watch again, then checked the clock above him. 'And' – he said, pausing to let the second hand tick up to twelve – 'stop writing please!'

I clicked my pen-top on to my ink pen, and leant back in my chair, sighing with relief. Ahead of me, Luci was scratching her head in a worried way.

'Stop writing, I said, Luci!' barked Mr Bronan from the front of the hall, looking at her menacingly.

Exaggeratedly, Luci flung down her pen. I exchanged a smile with Sadie, across the aisle from me. Thank goodness it'd gone well! I'd written an essay on Elizabeth that was OK, and I was pretty sure I'd got most of the multi-choice questions right on the rest of the topics we'd done.

'Nightmare!' said Luci, coming up to meet Sadie and Pippa and me, as we waited for her outside the hall afterwards. 'I really blew that one! How did yours go, Ella?'

'All right,' I nodded steadily.

'Great stuff!' She hugged me.

As we walked along the corridor, Pippa said, 'That

question about the names of Henry the Eighth's wives . . .' She frowned. 'I got five. But I couldn't think of the last one for the life of me.'

'Catherine of Aragon, Anne Boleyn, Jane Seymour–' I rattled off.

'Jane Seymour!' Pippa put her hand to her head. 'That was it! I completely forgot! I had to make one up instead!'

Luci glanced at Sadie and me mischievously before saying, 'You made one up, Pips? What did you put?'

'Oh – ' Pippa suddenly looked vague. 'Anita of London, or something,' she mumbled.

'*Anita*?' Luci burst into peals of laughter. 'Oh, Pippa!'

Pippa looked at her sulkily. 'So? I knew it wasn't *quite* right.'

As we were passing the library door, a thought struck me.

'My notes!' I said, grabbing Sadie's sleeve. 'Hang on here a minute; I'll just go and get them.'

Five minutes later, Sadie came into the library to look for me. I was scrabbling around, looking on the floor in the dustiest corners.

'I can't find them.' I knelt up and scratched my head. 'That's very odd.'

Sadie shrugged. 'Perhaps they fell on the floor and got thrown away when the cleaners came round.'

'Yes, you're probably right.'

'And it doesn't matter now, does it? The exam's over.' Sadie smiled, and held out her hand to pull me up. 'Come on. Let's go.'

Twelve

Luci ran to click off the tape recorder, and we all looked at Carlos in anticipation. He was standing leaning back against the studio mirror, his arms folded across his chest.

Slowly, he began to nod. 'It is not bad, ladies – not bad at all!'

I saw Luci grin with relief.

'Apart,' said Carlos, 'from that mess in the middle.' Everyone turned to Pippa, who blushed.

'But my opinion is' – Carlos flashed us a smile – 'yes, you have done very well!'

'Does that mean it'll go in the show?' Luci asked eagerly.

Carlos nodded again. 'That will be my recommendation.'

'Ace!' Luci looked round at the rest of us in delight. But Carlos held up his hand.

'Do not forget. You have two weeks still. Two weeks of hard rehearsing ahead, ladies.'

Luci laughed and slapped me on the back so hard it made me cough. 'Don't wor – oh, sorry Ella – don't worry, Carlos; I won't let 'em slack!'

Carlos strode across the studio to the door. As he opened it, he turned back to face us. 'And of course I shall want to see a run-through again next week,' he said, and left.

'Well done, Luci!' I gave her a hug.

'Yes,' added Pippa, studying her own reflection as she tried out one of her steps again. 'You know, Luci – it's actually quite a good piece.'

Luci clutched her chest with a sudden look of pain and staggered backwards. 'A compliment from Pippa! No – I can't bear it! Too – much of a – shock!'

And, as the rest of us collapsed in giggles, she collapsed on the floor.

All that week, every time I laid my head on my pillow after lights-out, I seemed to be haunted by the ticking clock.

'You may turn over!'

'You have one hour and fifteen minutes – begin!'

'Put your pens down!'

'And – stop writing!'

I imagined myself permanently in the hall, racing to finish my last essay or diagram, while Mr Bronan, or Mrs Sykes, or Miss Marks counted off the last seconds on their watch.

Luckily, in the real exams, I had no major disasters. My French paper wasn't quite faultless, I knew, and I'd done better English essays in class, but all in all, as I told my friends the night after our last exam:

'I did as well as I could.'

Luci, sitting next to me on my bed, squeezed my hand. 'Great! That's definitely top of the class then!'

The big question left, though, was: how had Guy done?

For most of this year, he hadn't cared two hoots about his school work; he'd been in more detentions than probably anyone else in our class; and I knew that his work, when he'd bothered to do it at all, hadn't been very good. It was probably only his dancing that had kept him from joining the list of people being asked to leave. But this meant I had no idea of how good his school work could be when he really tried. He'd been answering lots of questions correctly in class this term. What if he came out top in the exams?

'At least now the exams are over we can concentrate on this gala better,' said Sadie from the floor, where she was lying on her back doing leg-stretching exercises.

'When do we get our exam results?' asked Pippa.

'I heard Josie asking Mr Bronan that this morning,' said Luci. 'Next Monday, he said.'

'And what about the scholarship?' Pippa turned to me. 'Is that right at the end of term?'

I shook my head. 'They put up a notice on the board yesterday. There's going to be some sort of presentation assembly next Wednesday.'

'What? The same day as the gala?'

I nodded. 'No consideration for my nerves, eh?'

But nerves weren't really my worry. What I couldn't face was the idea that, if Guy got the scholarship, I'd have to dance with him that night on stage – and try to look happy while I was doing it. It didn't bear thinking about.

Thirteen

The next Monday morning, we all looked at Mr Bronan with particular attention as he drew out a fat red file from his briefcase and leafed through it.

'Right,' he said at last, laying the file open on his desk and looking up at us. 'I'm going to give you your exam results in a moment. But first, Gabriella Bruni?'

'Yes, Mr Bronan?' I half-rose from my seat. For once, Mr Bronan, who was usually really friendly to me, looked at me sourly.

'You are to go to Miss Stretton's office immediately,' he said brusquely.

'But my results–' I began. I'd been waiting for this moment for days. I couldn't bear to miss hearing what I'd got.

'Your exams are what Miss Stretton wishes to see you about,' Mr Bronan snapped. 'Now hurry up.'

A cold hand gripped my heart as I left the classroom and started off down the corridor towards Miss Stretton's office. Had I failed my exams outright? Surely not – I had been convinced they'd gone well; could I really have been so badly mistaken?

My hand trembled as I knocked on Miss Stretton's door.

'Are these your notes?' Miss Stretton held up a single sheet of file paper between her finger and thumb.

Immediately I recognised it: one of the two pages of history notes that had gone missing the night before our first exam.

'Yes!' I gasped. 'Where did you find it? I lost–'

'It's no use lying to me, Gabriella,' Miss Stretton snapped. 'I know exactly what happened.'

She gave me a significant look, as if I should know what this meant. I was utterly confused.

'What . . . what *did* happen, Miss Stretton?' I asked.

Miss Stretton fixed me with a steely glare. 'Do not play the innocent with me, child. You hoped to be awarded the Beckwith Medal, that I understand – and so you wanted to guarantee success in these exams. But to achieve success through *lies*, through *deceit* and *deception* –'

Miss Stretton spat out each of these horrible words as if they were bitter pips in something she was eating.

'I am disappointed in you, Gabriella. I took you for an honest, well brought-up girl.'

'Where did you find the notes?' I said in a tiny voice. It was all I could manage.

Miss Stretton sighed heavily. 'You insist on keeping up this charade of innocence! It won't wash with me, my girl!' She tapped the paper. 'This page of your revision notes – and you have already freely admitted that they *are* yours – '

I nodded.

' – were found in amongst the exam papers collected after your History exam. Clearly, your plan for cheating was not well-executed. Having smuggled these notes into the exam room, you then made the mistake of handing them in with your answers–'

'No!' I said quickly. 'No, Miss Stretton!'

'You are accusing *me* of lying?' Miss Stretton looked at me menacingly.

I swallowed, and said carefully, 'It might have looked as if that was what happened, Miss Stretton. But I didn't take any notes into the exam with me. I lost those notes before the exam. Ask my friends! They'll tell you – I was searching everywhere for them the night before.'

'I'm sure they will say that,' said Miss Stretton with an unfriendly smile. 'Having been told to do so by you. I have had many years' experience of dealing with children your age, Gabriella. I know that they have a natural propensity to lie when they have been caught doing wrong.'

I felt myself blush scarlet. My palms were sweaty and I could barely breathe.

'I didn't,' I murmured. 'Miss Stretton – I didn't cheat.'

'Enough, child!' Miss Stretton snapped, her eyes burning into me. She sighed impatiently. 'I need hardly tell you that this matter will be brought to the attention of the Scholarship Committee when they consider your application.'

The Scholarship Committee! My heart lurched. This was worse than if I'd failed my exams altogether. If the Committee really believed I'd been cheating, they'd never give me the scholarship in a million years.

'No! Miss Stretton!' I blurted, rushing right up to her desk and gripping the edge of it desperately. 'Please! Tell them I didn't do it –'

Miss Stretton looked at me, stony-faced. Then she opened a drawer, plucked out a wooden ruler, and tapped it smartly on my fingers. 'Off! Off!' she said. I let go of the desk.

'You may go,' said Miss Stretton thinly.

It was like some terrible dream in which, however loud you shouted, no one could hear you.

I turned away from Miss Stretton. The room seemed to be swaying, as if I was on board a ship. As I headed for the door, I staggered and had to clutch at a chair as I passed.

I was sure I heard Miss Stretton snort behind me. She probably thought it was just another piece of acting.

Fourteen

'Hang on, hang on!' Luci jumped off the low playground wall she'd been balancing on and faced me squarely. 'Are you trying to say Miss Stretton thinks you *cheated*?'

On either side of her, Sadie and Pippa were staring at me in disbelief.

I nodded. 'It was one of those pages of notes I lost . . .' I hesitated, still unable to believe it. 'Miss Stretton said they'd been found in amongst the exam papers.'

Pippa shook her head in wonder. 'It's funny that you could have taken them into the hall, and then handed them in by mistake, all without realising it.'

'Pippa!' Luci turned on her savagely, making Pippa start back in shock. 'Don't be stupid! Ella *didn't* take the notes into the exam, and she *didn't* put them in amongst the papers!'

'So just how did they get there, then, clever clogs?' asked Pippa defiantly.

'That's what we've got to find out.' Luci fixed me with a determined look.

'Someone must have put them there deliberately,' said Sadie, frowning. 'I just can't imagine–'

'Who'd want to do that?' Luci finished for her. Then she shook her head. 'Me neither.'

I slumped back to sit on the wall, and looked up at my three friends. 'Thanks for believing me,' I said. 'If *you* didn't, I don't know what I'd do.'

'Of course we believe you!' exclaimed Sadie. 'We've just got to find a way to get Miss Stretton to, as well.' She sighed heavily. 'After all that hard work you did! All those weeks.'

'We must fight to clear your name!' said Luci, pounding her fist into her other hand. 'I'll go to Miss Stretton now and tell her!'

'It's no good, Luci,' I started up and grabbed Luci's sleeve. 'I told Miss Stretton she could ask you three to back up my story. But she already thinks you'll just lie to protect me.'

Luci flung her hands up. 'That woman! She thinks the worst of everyone!'

I sighed. 'I can't blame her. It looks so obvious, doesn't it? Everything points to me – *I'd* even think I did it, if I was her.'

'We'll just have to find out who really did it ourselves, and then go to the teachers,' said Pippa.

I sighed. It looked like an impossible mountain to climb. Then a thought struck me. 'How were the exam results? I guess Mr Bronan didn't read out anything for me?'

Sadie shook her head. 'He missed you out altogether. We three all passed everything, though.'

'Me only just,' said Luci sheepishly.

Pippa drew herself up proudly. 'I got seventy-two per cent in English.'

'Well done!' I mustered a smile for her. I really was pleased. I knew Pippa had worked hard to make up for having done so little at the beginning of the year.

I hardly dared ask my next question. 'Can anyone remember what Guy got?'

Sadie frowned. 'Erm . . . I'm afraid he did really well. I can't remember the exact results . . . but the lowest was sixty-seven, I think – and I'm sure he got a couple in the eighties.'

My heart sank. Things were looking worse and worse for me.

Suddenly, Luci slapped a hand to her forehead. 'Stupid me!' she cried. 'Of course!'

'What?' We all looked at her.

'That's who did it! Don't you see? The only person with a motive.'

'Who?'

'Guy Jenkins, of course!' She looked about her, then lowered her voice. 'He's going in for the scholarship, right? And he knows he can't possibly beat Ella, because she's so brilliant and works so hard and everything. So – what does he do? He steals Ella's notes – he was always in the library when we were working there, remember? Then he smuggles them into the exam, and slips them into the pile of exam papers when they're collected in. Bingo!' She clapped her hands.

It sounded all too likely. Luci was right: who else would have a motive to mess up my exams except Guy? When the bell rang for the end of break and we followed everyone else back indoors, Sadie spotted him, standing with Alex and Vaz over on the far side of the corridor.

'Look – there he is!'

'Right –' said Luci, breaking away from us and pushing her way across the tide of people heading towards their different classrooms.

'Luci, don't!' I called after her. 'You can't just accuse him like–'

But I was too late.

'Hey, Guy!' I heard Luci shout.

Sadie, Pippa and I followed her, then hung back, listening. We saw Guy turn. 'What d'you want, Croc?'

He called Luci 'Croc' because she's Australian – on account of *Crocodile Dundee*. She didn't find it funny at the best of times.

Now she stumped up to him and jabbed her finger into his shoulder. 'You stole Ella's history notes, didn't you? And put them in with the exam papers! Admit it!'

Guy brushed Luci's hand away roughly and laughed. 'Trying to turn supersleuth are you? Zero out of ten, Croc. I never saw any notes, let alone nicked them. Go pester someone else.' He turned back to his friends.

'Oh no you don't!' Luci screamed, running round to the front of him to bar his way. 'I won't let you get away with it, you creep! Just because you don't stand a chance against her for the scholarship–'

Guy pushed her out of the way, but Luci pushed

back. Then Guy pushed again, and soon it had turned into a shoving match.

'Luci! No!' I ran towards her.

'Just what is going on here?' Mr Bronan's voice barked from beyond the huddle. Everyone turned to look at him. 'All-in wrestling bout is it, Jenkins?' He grabbed Guy by the collar and pulled him to one side. Then he turned to Luci. 'And Luci Simpson? Well, well – what a pair! You should have sold tickets. We could all have enjoyed the spectacle. Never mind. Perhaps you'll enjoy detention nearly as much.'

'But Mr Bro–' began Luci.

'Shut it!' He pointed a finger at her, then swung it round to Guy too. 'Both of you. Lunchtime. In Room Three. Right?'

'Yes, Mr Bronan,' Guy and Luci muttered together.

With a grunt of satisfaction, Mr Bronan stalked on down the corridor.

'Thanks for nothing.' Guy looked daggers at Luci, then loped off with Alex and Vaz.

Luci dusted down her blazer and came back to join us.

'Sorry about the detention,' I said.

'You're sorry?' Luci looked at me quizzically.

I nodded. 'If it wasn't for me –'

'Aw, no worries. It's only a lunchtime. Listen –' She looked at me keenly. 'Guy's definitely the one. I'm telling you – he had this shifty look in his eyes.'

'But if he won't admit it, what do we do?' asked Sadie.

Luci scratched her head and grimaced. 'Proof! That's what we need!'

'And fast,' I said. 'The Scholarship Committee makes its decision the day after tomorrow, remember.'

'It doesn't give us much time,' admitted Sadie. 'Talking of which' – she glanced at the clock – 'we'd better get a move on or Mrs Sykes'll put us all in detention.'

We started walking down the corridor.

'Fingerprints!' said Luci suddenly. We stopped and looked at her.

'Like on TV cop shows,' she said. 'You know – the detective goes in with gloves on or something and dusts the room for fingerprints. That's how she catches the criminal.'

'So?' Pippa frowned.

'So,' Luci made a face as if we were all being really slow. 'If Guy stole Ella's notes from that table in the library, there must be his fingerprints there, loads of them!'

'Yes – as well as ours, and all the other people who've sat there every day since then –' said Pippa.

Luci's shoulders slumped. 'Spoil sports,' she said. 'It sounded really exciting to me.' We set off walking again.

I shook my head. 'It's impossible. I may as well accept it now: I'm not going to get that scholarship. I just have to try and make the most of my last term at the Evanova.'

'No!' Luci ran in front of me. 'Don't say that!' She

took hold of both my arms, and gave me a shake. 'Don't say that, Ella! We're going to crack this one. By hook or by crook.'

Fifteen

That afternoon, it was our last rehearsal for the gala before moving into the theatre for the dress rehearsal the next day. Miss Latimer took us all together, boys and girls, in Dempsey Studio.

Usually, I got on well with Miss Latimer. But the weird thing was, today, she ignored me completely. Every time her face turned in my direction, it was as if she was looking straight through me. It was awful; I thought I would have preferred her to shout at me – if only she'd said *something*.

'Guy – make sure you're just a little further to the right when Melanie and David run on to the stage,' she instructed, when she really meant Guy and me, because we were standing together.

'Next time you're throwing wild, stupid accusations about,' hissed Guy as we shifted our positions obediently, 'have the courage to face me yourself, OK? Don't go sending your brainless friends–'

'I never sent–'

'Guy!' Miss Latimer snapped. 'Stop talking! We haven't a moment to waste today!'

That evening, before supper, Luci summoned us all to her bedroom for a planning meeting. It was a miserable affair. No one had any idea of what to do next.

'You know the strange thing?' I said at last, looking through the little window above Luci's bed to the trees outside.

'Hm?' Luci roused herself from her thoughts.

I turned back to face her. 'It's that one of those pages of notes is still missing. Miss Stretton only had one page. But I lost two. If we knew where the second one was, it might be some sort of clue.'

In a second, Luci blazed into life. 'Brilliant!' she cried, bouncing off the bed. 'That's the evidence we need! If Guy still has that second page – it's proof he did it.'

'I bet he does have it somewhere.' Sadie nodded slowly.

'We should look for it,' said Luci.

'Where?' I asked.

Sadie shrugged. 'His locker? That's the first place I'd think of –'

'Right,' said Luci. 'Think of a time when he won't be there – and I'll go and look.'

'Go to the boys' dormitory?' said Pippa, aghast. 'Luci, we're not allowed!'

'Oh, forget that!' Luci flapped a hand in the air. 'This is Ella's place at the school that's at stake here! It's far too important to worry about silly rules.'

'I won't let you get into trouble on my account,' I said, much more firmly than I felt. 'If anyone's going, it should be me.'

'OK, then we'll both go,' said Luci.

'Me too!' said Sadie, scrambling to her feet. 'All for one and one for all!'

There was a pause. Pippa noticed that there were three faces looking at her. 'What?' she said irritably. Luci raised her eyebrows.

'Oh, all right then,' Pippa sighed. Then she wagged a finger at Luci. 'But if we get into trouble, I'm going to say it was your idea.'

'When?' Sadie interrupted, looking at her watch. 'We can't do it now; we're meant to be down in the dining hall in ten minutes.'

Luci frowned in thought. 'Well, I heard Vaz saying earlier that there's a footie match on tonight. I bet you the boys will all be in the TV room after supper. Their dormitory should be empty.'

Sadie rubbed her hands together. 'Perfect!'

Sixteen

'What was that?' Pippa stopped suddenly and cocked her head on one side, like a rabbit, listening.

'What?' whispered Luci, almost cannoning into her.

'I heard footsteps! There!'

'That was me, you idiot! Now hurry up – we haven't got all night.'

It was really weird, creeping into a bit of the school we'd never been in before. You'd think, after nearly a year at the Evanova, we'd know every inch of the building. But this was completely new territory.

'What's in there?' I pointed to our left.

Sadie pushed the door open a crack and poked her head round it. 'A washroom,' she said, coming back out again. 'We can't be far off!'

'What if Pondsnail finds us?' asked Pippa nervously. Pondsnail was Mrs Pondswell, the fearsome junior boys' matron.

'We'll say . . .' Luci hesitated. 'We'll say . . . Well, we'll think of something I'm sure.'

'Aha! Look,' said Sadie. 'That's the senior boys' dorm. I'm sure I've heard the boys in our year say theirs is directly above.'

'And here's the staircase,' added Luci, as she reached the next corner. 'Come on!'

We hurried up the stairs, treading as quietly as we

could, and sure enough, on the floor above we came to a door marked 'Junior Boys'. My heart was thudding so hard I thought it might burst, but still, I told myself I should lead the way.

I turned the handle and pushed on the door, then felt round for a light switch.

'No' – Luci stuck out her hand and pulled mine back. 'Don't turn it on! You can see these windows from the corridor down by the Old Library, remember?' She looked round the shadowy room. 'I reckon there's just about enough light left, anyway, if we hurry.'

The four of us piled into the room and shut the door behind us.

'Right,' said Luci, taking charge. 'Sadie, you stay by the door, and listen out for footsteps. Ella' – she turned to me – 'you and I'll do the searching. You know what your notes look like after all.'

'Oh, leave me out why don't you?' Pippa huffed.

Luci sighed. 'Pippa – you can help us, OK?'

I looked down the long room, with the beds in rows on either side, and identical white lockers standing sentry beside each one. 'How do we know which is Guy's, then?'

'Check the dressing gowns,' instructed Luci. 'They're all supposed to have name tags in, right?'

I nodded. 'Good thinking.'

Swiftly, Luci, Pippa and I ran up to a bed each, and grabbed the dressing gown that was folded neatly on the pillow. 'Pondsnail must be a real stickler for this folding business,' whispered Luci. 'We'd better be careful to put them back neatly.'

It was the folding that took the time.

'Ah!' I whispered a few minutes later. At last I'd found it. The name-tape on this dressing gown was half coming off, and had curled up, but I spotted '–nkins' and, smoothing it out and tilting it towards the window to catch the fading light, the rest of the name revealed itself.

'G. R. E.,' read Pippa over my shoulder. 'I wonder what his middle names are?'

I folded the dressing gown up again, and tried the door of his locker. It wouldn't budge. 'Of course!' I whispered in anguish. 'It's locked! What do we do now?'

Luci looked unperturbed. 'No worries,' she said, coming round the bed to join us. 'There are only a few places people hide keys. Trust me.'

Quickly, she lifted the edge of the mattress and felt underneath. She shook her head. Then she pulled out Guy's slippers from beneath the bed and felt inside them. Nothing again.

Then, hitching up her skirt, Luci hauled herself on top of the locker and felt along the top edge of the window frame. 'Gotcha!'

She came down brandishing a small silver key and tried it in the locker door. It turned smoothly and the door swung open.

'Jeepers, what's all this junk?' Luci rummaged swiftly, pulling papers out and peering at them, then stuffing them back inside again with a shake of her head. 'Nothing!' she said at last. 'I can't believe–'

'Footsteps!' came Sadie's urgent whisper from the doorway.

I looked at Luci in panic. 'Pondsnail!' she said, her eyes wide. 'Quick! Under the beds!' Then she flung herself out flat and rolled under Guy's bed. I saw Sadie, by a bed near the door, duck down to do the same. I followed suit.

'Pippa!' Luci hissed. We could all hear the footsteps now. 'Get down!'

From my place under the bed next to Luci's, I could see Pippa's feet – and then her knees and hands as she knelt down gingerly. 'But it'll be all dusty–' she began.

'For Pete's sake just get down, will you?' Luci's hand shot out and tugged at her skirt.

'Get off!' Pippa hissed. But she did as she was told and slid under a bed.

We all held our breath.

A minute later, the dormitory door opened, and the light flicked on. I could picture Mrs Pondswell standing in the doorway, looking grumpily round the room. Had Luci shut Guy's locker? I didn't dare move my head to check.

I waited for the light to flick off and the door to shut again.

The door did shut, but the light was still on. With a lurch I realised that Mrs Pondswell was still in the room. Footsteps came towards me: the rasping footsteps of those rubbery soles you get on sensible lace-ups. Just the sort of shoes Mrs Pondswell would go for.

The footsteps stopped at the foot of the bed I was under. My blood pounded in my head. Swivelling my eyes, I could just see one of the shoes. Yes, sensible brown lace-ups. But – hang on a minute – they looked an awful lot smaller than I would have expected. Did Mrs Pondswell have tiny feet? I'd never noticed before.

I was just considering this, when the feet disappeared and, with a creak of springs, the bed above curved down towards me. As I wondered whether I was going to be squashed completely, a face suddenly appeared, upside down, about four inches from mine.

'Oh! Hello!' it said. 'I had a funny feeling there was someone under here.'

Luci told me later that I squeaked in fright, but I can't remember it.

What I do remember is that the next minute, I'd pulled myself out from under the bed and was on my feet, face to face with David Wilder.

David was kneeling on his bed, calmly surveying the three other faces that had popped up from other beds around him.

'Don't you have a mirror in this room?' asked Pippa tetchily, casting about for somewhere to check her reflection, and patting her hair as she did so.

David didn't reply. Instead he gave a friendly grin and asked a question of his own. 'Are you going to tell me what you're doing here, then, or is it some secret operation?'

I hesitated, so Luci came to my aid.

'Secret operation, really,' she said. 'But you may as well know.' She sat on Guy's bed. 'We're looking for something Guy stole from Ella.'

'Some revision notes,' I put in.

'Something to do with that cheating business?' asked David mildly.

'Yeah,' said Luci. 'Except it wasn't cheating. Not on Ella's part anyway. Guy stole two sheets of her notes and planted one in amongst the exam papers.'

'We *think* he did,' I said cautiously.

'It must have been him,' said Luci firmly. 'So, anyway, if we can find the other page amongst Guy's things–'

'It's evidence,' finished David. 'I see.'

'Do you know he did it?' asked Sadie.

David shook his head. 'No idea. To be honest, he doesn't talk to me that mu–' He stopped, suddenly alert.

'What?' mouthed Luci.

'I heard something!' David whispered. 'Quick! You'd better get back.'

In a flash we were all four under the beds. This time Pippa didn't hesitate. And it was a good job – because we were only just in time.

'David!' snapped Mrs Pondswell's unmistakeable voice from the direction of the doorway. 'What are you doing?'

'Just reading, Mrs Pondswell,' I heard David say above me. 'I wasn't interested in the football match, so –'

'Humph.' Mrs Pondswell grunted. 'Was there somebody else here just now? I could have sworn I heard voices –'

'Oh - er –' David hesitated. 'I read out loud to myself, Mrs Pondswell,' he said at last.

'Babyish habit!'

'Yes, Mrs Pondswell.'

Then the door shut with a click and we heard footsteps receding down the corridor.

'All clear,' David whispered.

'Thanks,' I said, pulling myself out from under his bed again and dusting myself down.

'Yeah, we owe you one,' said Luci, emerging beside me.

'Look,' David checked his watch. 'You'd better scarper actually. The match is almost over and some of the others are bound to come up here afterwards.'

'Right. Well,' Luci turned the key in the door of Guy's locker, and then climbed back up to the window to return it to its place. 'Nothing there, anyhow. We're going to have to think again.'

'Thanks, David,' I said as we left. 'And thanks to you lot, too,' I added, as Luci, Sadie, Pippa and I hurried back along the corridor. 'It was worth a try.'

In front of me, Luci shook her head. 'This isn't over,' she said. 'Not by a long chalk.'

Part Four

Ella's Last Dance?

Seventeen

As if the weather could sense how things were going for me, the next day dawned as grey and miserable as an English summer day could. Time was running out. It was the day before the gala performance – and the day before the Scholarship Committee would announce its decision.

Moreover, we were going to have precious little of the day to ourselves; straight after lunch, we were due at the Grand Theatre in Wittingham for the gala dress rehearsal.

'What are you doing?' I said to Luci when we were on the coach. She was kneeling up in her seat, facing backwards, her eyes peculiarly fixed.

Luci didn't even blink as she answered. 'I'm staring Guy Jenkins out. I'm going to put so much pressure on him, he'll have to confess.'

'Luci Simpson!' Miss Marks's voice cut above the chatter. 'Sit down, for goodness' sake!'

Luci sighed and did as she was told.

'Ella' – the next minute she leant round the side of her seat to look back at me – 'don't worry, OK? I mean – don't let this whole business get in the way of your performance. This should be a great show for you.'

'Yes.' I nodded. 'My last one.'

'No!' Pippa prodded me. 'Don't say that! I won't allow it!'

I knew my friends were being kind, trying not to let me lose hope. But they were just kidding themselves. They were avoiding the truth – and what good did that do?

When we got to the theatre, it was completely overrun with Evanova pupils. Henry, the stage door man, shook his head in wonder as we filed past him. 'More of you? I don't believe it!'

Miss Featherstone was standing in the hallway, clutching three different clipboards.

'*Third* formers on the *fourth* floor – *fourth* formers on the *second* . . .'

The first years had been stuck in two dressing rooms on the top floor of the building – one room for the boys and one for the girls.

'At least we don't have to share, like we did at Christmas!' sniffed Pippa, when we got there.

Over the dressing-room tannoy crackled a muddle of voices. Occasionally I could make out Miss Latimer's. 'Not purple, Evelyn. Madame simply hates purple.'

'Is Madame here?' I heard Rachel Cooper ask behind me.

'No, silly,' said Melanie. 'The whole thing's in honour of her, right? So she won't see anything till the performance tomorrow. It's sort of like a surprise.'

'I heard the second years saying someone from the fifth is going to do that solo from *Giselle* – the one Madame was really famous for,' Josie Wells said, and did a twirl in the middle of the room that knocked over two chairs.

'That's enough, Josie!' said Miss Marks, who looked as if she was beginning to regret offering to chaperone us today. 'Shouldn't you girls be changing into costume, or something?'

Half an hour later I was ready. I smoothed my hands over the net of my beautiful blue tutu, and checked my hair in the mirror. Just then Luci bounded across to me from the other side of the room.

'What are you doing, Ella? You're in the wrong costume! We have "Dreamers" first, not "Waltz of the Flowers".'

'Oh, yes.' I looked down at myself in surprise. My mind had been completely elsewhere.

'Come on – come on!' Luci started undoing the hooks and eyes on the back of my tutu. 'We'll be late!'

'Well, Carlos looked quite pleased,' said Sadie, as we climbed the long flights of stairs up from the stage after our 'Dreamers' run-through.

'You're still going too far to the left when you do your three *pas de bourrées*, Pippa,' said Luci, coming up behind us.

Pippa didn't answer. Instead she said. 'Did you see that man Miss Stretton was with?'

'Which man?' said Sadie.

'I didn't even see Miss Stretton,' I mumbled.

'Yes – I did!' said Luci. 'About halfway back on the left. She had this man beside her.' Luci puffed out her cheeks. 'Big guy. 'Bout this tall' – she held her hand high in the air – 'in a great big overcoat.'

Sadie giggled. 'Do you think it's Miss Stretton's boyfriend?'

That thought made the others laugh. Then Luci shook her head. 'He looked really important to me.'

'Well,' Pippa pushed on the dressing-room door. 'Better get changed for "Flowers".'

Ten minutes later, when I was back in my tutu, there was a knock on the door.

'Come in!' called Miss Marks.

It was Lorraine, one of the second year girls. 'Where's Gabriella Bruni?'

I stood up. 'Here!'

'Miss Stretton wants to see you,' said Lorraine. 'She's in the Green Room.'

'What for?'

Lorraine shrugged.

Luci grabbed my arm. 'Hey! My telepathy!' she whispered eagerly. 'It worked! Guy's confessed . . .'

'Don't be silly,' said Pippa, at my other side. Then she frowned. 'But Miss Stretton could have found out it was him.'

'She'd wait till we got back to school to say anything.' I shook my head.

Luci winked. 'Miss Stretton's mind works in mysterious ways, we all know that.'

Sadie was skipping up and down with excitement. 'What else could it be? Oh, Ella – you must be in the clear!'

I laughed. I could hardly believe it. 'I'd better go,' I said. 'We'll be on for "Flowers" soon.'

I was all ready except for my pointe shoes. For speed, I just slipped on my outdoor shoes and ran out into the corridor.

'Yes, go. Hurry!' said Luci behind me. 'Oh, I knew it would all be OK in the end!'

'I agree, Mrs Pondswell,' came Miss Stretton's voice. 'But I have spoken to Miss Latimer already. I will deal with it now. Thank you for bringing this matter to my attention.'

As I slipped into the Green Room, Mrs Pondswell passed me on her way out. She gave me a sour look. I wondered what she'd been talking to Miss Stretton about.

The door clicked shut behind me. I stood facing Miss Stretton. In a room of easy chairs and sofas, she'd found the one hard, wooden, high-backed chair, and was sitting on that, as stiffly as ever. Her feet were neatly together, her back absolutely straight.

'Well, Gabriella,' she began crisply. 'This time you have excelled yourself.'

I frowned. I didn't know what she meant. Was she saying I'd danced well? Her voice didn't sound at all friendly – I didn't think it could possibly be a compliment.

She held up a crumpled piece of paper. 'I have it, you see? Guy Jenkins, when he found it, gave it straight to Mrs Pondswell, and she has brought it straight to me.'

'What is it?' I asked.

Somehow, without smiling, Miss Stretton managed to let out a hollow laugh. 'But of course! You have this habit of pretending to have forgotten your own actions, Gabriella, don't you? Let me help you out, this time. Let me read you the note that you left for Guy Jenkins.'

I listened in consternation as Miss Stretton read from the paper she was holding.

'Guy – You have no right to that scholarship – it is mine. Don't try to stand in my way. I'm warning you. If you get it, horrible things will happen to you.'

I gasped. 'That's awful!'

Miss Stretton stared at me coldly. 'It is indeed. Why, then, Gabriella, did you write it?'

'Miss Stretton, I didn't!'

Miss Stretton stood up and, stepping towards me, turned the paper around and held it in front of my face.

'Is this not your handwriting?'

I could hardly believe my eyes. 'It – it does look ever so like it,' I stammered truthfully. 'But it isn't! It can't be! I would never write anything so horrible!'

'Lies, lies, lies!' snapped Miss Stretton, whipping the paper away again. 'Even when I have the evidence in my hands you will not tell the truth!'

'You – you don't understand,' I managed to stammer.

'Oh, I understand very well,' said Miss Stretton savagely. 'I understand what a nasty, wicked little girl you really are!'

I couldn't say any more. It was as if my tongue had shrivelled up in my mouth like a dry autumn leaf. Miss Stretton's words seemed to swirl around my head: 'nasty' . . . 'wicked' . . . I couldn't bear the idea that someone thought of me like that, but what could I do, when she wouldn't listen to a word I said?

'Yes, you may well cry – now,' said Miss Stretton, looking at me coldly.

I hadn't even realised that I was – but when I raised my hand to my cheek, I felt that it was wet.

'I'm surprised at you, Gabriella, I really am.' Miss Stretton paused. 'Naturally, I feel you have absolutely no right to appear in this gala. It is a privilege that should be denied you. But, having spoken to Miss Latimer, I understand that it is too late to replace you, and that if you dropped out, it would spoil things for others. For Guy himself, in fact, the victim of your unpleasantness.'

I stared at Miss Stretton in disbelief. She met my gaze calmly.

'I hardly need tell you that this matter will be brought

to the attention of the Scholarship Committee.'

'No, Miss Stretton.' I knew what that meant. If there had been any chance left for me at all, it had vanished completely.

'To be perfectly frank, though you are a promising dancer, Gabriella, I shall be glad to be rid of you from this school. I do not like the thought of such dishonest, spiteful people walking our corridors.'

I stared down at my hands and touched them to my beautiful blue skirt. They were trembling.

'That is all I have to say to you.' Miss Stretton stood up again abruptly. 'Go now.'

'Yes, Miss Stretton,' I murmured, and hurried to the door.

The dressing room was deserted. I flung myself into my chair and looked at my reflection in the mirror. Black streaks of eyeliner had coursed down my face, and above them, my eyes stared hollowly back at me. I felt utterly empty.

Suddenly, my ears tuned in to the sounds coming over the tannoy. I heard Miss Latimer's voice faintly, 'Well, where is she?' Then the unmistakeable Australian twang of Luci's voice, 'I don't know. She had to go and see Miss Stretton.'

They were on stage already for 'Waltz of the Flowers'! Hastily, I rubbed the smeared eyeliner off my cheeks and kicked off my outdoor shoes. Then I rummaged in my bag.

My pointe shoes . . . where were they? In desperation, I picked up my bag and tipped all its contents into a heap on the floor. Tights, hairbrush, grips, pins and ribbons cascaded down. But no pointe shoes. I looked on the floor under my chair. Not there.

Over the tannoy, I heard the 'Waltz of the Flowers' music start up. I had no option. I grabbed my soft ballet shoes, pulled them on, and crossed and knotted the ribbons as quickly as I could. Then I raced from the dressing room and down the stairs.

The stage, when I got there, was a mass of moving bodies, as the whole of my year went through their steps, weaving in and out of one another in time to the music. Guy was at the front, dancing on his own with a gap beside him where I should have been. Hastily, I made my way through to him.

'Sorry . . . oh! sorry,' I found myself saying as people cannoned into me. At last I got to Guy. I didn't want to look at him. I just took his hand and picked up in the middle of the sequence he was dancing.

'Stop! Stop!' Miss Latimer screeched above the sound of the piano. Mr Judd halted.

'Gabriella. Your pointe shoes. Where are they?'

'I –' Appalled, I heard my voice tremble. I would not cry in front of everyone. I wouldn't . . .

'I don't know, Miss Latimer.'

'What do you mean, you don't know?' Miss Latimer marched down the aisle to the front of the auditorium. 'Not only do you disrupt us all by being late, but you do not even have the common courtesy to arrive properly dressed.'

I snatched a sideways glance at Guy. He was looking

at me as if he hated my guts. My stomach tightened – not 'as if' – he *did* hate my guts. He thought I'd sent him that awful letter –

I couldn't help it. I burst into floods of tears.

'Oh, get on with it, you silly girl,' said Miss Latimer coldly, turning away. 'Pick it up from the phrase before please, Mr Judd –'

As the music started up again, Guy snatched my hand.

'Cry baby. Thought I'd be scared by a stupid note, did you?'

His voice seemed a long way away. As I danced, the tears kept coming, until the auditorium before me and the figures whirling around me blurred and merged together. This was a bad dream. It had to be.

Eighteen

When I told Sadie, Luci and Pippa about the awful letter and about my missing pointe shoes, they were as stunned and confused as I was. Everything seemed to have spun out of control and there was nothing any of us could do about it. I somehow hoped the next day just wouldn't come. But it did, of course. And, after our usual ballet lesson, the whole school gathered in the assembly hall for the announcement of the year's scholarship awards and prizes.

Mrs Seymour, head of the Scholarship Committee this year, was up on the stage, a sheaf of papers in her hand. Beside her sat the formidable figure of Madame in her wheelchair, who was going to hand the certificates to the pupils as they came up to collect their awards.

'Is it Madame's actual birthday today?' I heard Sadie whisper to Pippa. 'What with the gala being tonight and everything?'

'Not sure,' Pippa whispered back. 'I have a feeling her birthday's later in the summer. Could be wrong though.'

'We'll start with the Sixth Year,' Mrs Seymour said, once everyone was in, and the doors at the back of the hall had swung shut. 'As always, we have the Smith-Harrison Prize to award, which this year goes to Saskia Williams.'

The school burst into applause as, from the back of the hall, a tall slender girl with strawberry blonde hair made her way along the side aisle to the stage steps. She curtsied when Madame handed her her certificate, and bent forward respectfully to hear what Madame was saying. Then, blushing, she hurried back past us the way she had come.

'There are no scholarships in the Fifth Year,' went on Mrs Seymour. 'But in the Fourth Year we have two prizes, the Fidment Shields, for the most promising boy and girl –'

I watched as the pupils came up on to the stage, crossing to Madame one by one. Each time, the clapping rose to a crescendo and fell away again.

'The Third Year–' I heard Mrs Seymour say. More clapping. More figures coming and going.

'And the Second Year–' It felt like an astronaut's countdown.

'Finally,' Mrs Seymour said, looking up from her paper with a smile, 'there's only one scholarship in the first year this year: the Beckwith Medal. And I am very pleased to announce . . .'

Beside me, Pippa's hand felt for mine and squeezed it.

'That it has been awarded to . . .'

I shut my eyes and prayed for a miracle.

'. . . Guy Jenkins!'

Around us, the whole school burst into applause.

'Cheat!' hissed Luci at the other side of me. I looked at my feet and blinked hard. My chin was trembling.

When I looked up again, Guy was on the stage above me, grinning as Madame handed him his certificate, and the medal in its presentation box. Before he came back down the steps, he held the box up to the clapping school like a team captain with a football trophy.

'Can you *believe* it?' muttered Pippa under her breath.

On the way back to the classroom, I didn't say a word. There was nothing to say.

Josie Wells barged up to me. 'It's such a shame, Ella. You probably could have got it if you hadn't done those mean things.'

'Shut it, Josie.' Luci put a protective arm round my shoulder. 'You know full well she didn't.' But Josie had turned away.

As I entered the classroom, I saw Alex Brodie give Guy the high fives. 'Yeah! Well done, mate!'

Then Guy spotted me. He raised his medal as if he was toasting me, tauntingly. I looked away.

'But the letter proves it *can't* have been Guy who put my history notes in with the exam papers,' I said after lunch. It was a sunny day at last, and the four of us had made straight for our favourite spot by the beech tree.

'Are you kidding?' Luci shook her head vehemently. 'It's the oldest trick in the book, I'm telling you! He wrote that letter to himself!'

'The handwriting, though – it looked just like mine.'

Luci knelt up in the grass. 'But that fits in perfectly

too. You lost two pages of history notes, right? So if he still had one, he could've copied your writing from that. Simple!'

'Hmm,' said Pippa. 'He's certainly not the no-brain I always took him for.'

'We're going to sort it out. We *are*,' said Luci. 'But for today, Ella, you must forget it. Or it'll ruin the show for you. Today, just concentrate on the performance.'

But the feeling that I was in a bad dream still hadn't left me. I was finding it hard to concentrate on anything at all.

'Ella? Ella!' Pippa tapped me on the shoulder. 'Come on! You've got to pack your bag! The coach'll be downstairs in ten minutes!' We were up in our rooms after school, getting ready to go to the theatre.

'Oh – right.' Listlessly, I began putting together the things I needed for the performance – pink tights, hairbrush, hairpins . . .

'You need your spare pointe shoes, don't forget.'

I searched for them in the drawer. They were the older of my two pairs, too soft now from overuse. They'd be painful to dance in, but I had no choice.

'Come along, dear hearts!' Miss Lum, our matron, called from the far end of the corridor. 'You're coming with me today! Come along now!'

The coach journey into Wittingham was over all too quickly, and soon I was plunged into the mayhem of the theatre. Backstage was a whirl of excited chatter, the glare of the bare light bulbs fringing dressing-room mirrors, and glimpses of brightly patterned costumes and painted faces flushed with excitement. Everything seemed to rush past me too fast, as if I was on a merry-go-round that just wouldn't stop.

'You OK?' said Luci as she fixed my hair for 'Dreamers'. Since 'Waltz of the Flowers' wasn't until later in the programme, the rest of the girls in our dressing room had a long time to wait. They were still in their school uniforms, reading each other's good luck cards and posing for souvenir photos.

'I'm fine.' I nodded.

Luci twirled me round and looked at me sharply. 'Show them. Will you? Show the stupid Miss Strettons of this world what you can do. This is your big night, Ella. This is your–'

'Last dance,' I said.

'No,' said Luci sternly. 'That's exactly what it's not. But it *is* the first public performance of a piece of my choreography. I'm depending on you!' She poked me in the shoulder. 'Don't let me down!'

I smiled. 'Stop worrying. I'm fine.'

But I felt numb. I felt as if someone could have jabbed a great big needle into me and I wouldn't have felt a thing. I hoped my feet knew the steps of Luci's ballet by themselves – because it didn't feel like any messages from my brain could get as far as my toes tonight.

Over the tannoy, we heard the audience taking their seats – the buzz of conversation, the rustling of programmes and, soon, the strange sounds of the orchestra tuning up.

'Hey – aren't there loads of VIP guests tonight?' Josie Wells said, her eyes sparkling. 'People Madame's worked with. Someone said Amelia Beresford is flying in specially from New York.'

'No! Really?'

'I swear I heard some of the Fourth Years talking about it in the loos.'

'Come on, Ella.' Sadie tugged at my sleeve. 'Let's go down to the wings.'

'What?' I said. 'It's not time yet, surely.'

Pippa and Luci appeared behind Sadie. 'It's a bit early,' Luci agreed. 'But I'll tell Miss Lum I want to run through something in the hall downstairs. You look like you could do with a minute out of this madhouse.'

'How did it go, dear hearts?' asked Miss Lum when we came back into the dressing room, panting from all the stairs we'd just run up. 'I heard some wonderful applause just now. Was that for you?' She looked round at Luci, Sadie and Pippa, but avoided looking at me. I turned away. I couldn't bear the thought that dear Miss Lum believed all those horrid things about me, just like everyone else.

'Sure was!' said Luci. 'Thanks guys! You did me proud!'

Miss Lum smiled. 'No mistakes, then?'

'Well,' Luci looked sheepish. 'I was so busy trying to see what the audience were thinking, I missed one bit at the beginning. Pippa covered it up really well though.'

At that moment, Josie, who'd been leaning out into the corridor, popped her head back into the dressing room. 'Guess what? I just saw that Saskia girl – the one who got the prize this morning. She's in the most gorgeous costume – big white skirt – ' Josie fanned her hands out at her sides.

'She must be the one doing the *Giselle* solo!' exclaimed Melanie Cooper. 'Oh, can we go and watch her from the wings, Miss Lum?'

'Yes, can we? Please!' put in Josie, hurrying over to where Miss Lum stood.

'I'm afraid not, dears,' said Miss Lum sorrowfully. 'I have strict instructions that no one is to be allowed to watch anything they're not in. Just imagine! We'd end up with half the school crammed into the wings.'

'But Miss Lum–'

'I'm sorry, dears.' Miss Lum checked her watch. 'But there's a while to go yet until your piece, isn't there? How about popping down to the Green Room, eh? Mrs Sykes is in charge of laying on orange squash there, I'm told.'

From Josie and Melanie's faces it was quite clear that the prospect of orange squash was cold comfort for the disappointment of not being allowed to watch Saskia Williams dancing *Giselle*. But still, half a dozen voices piped up, 'We'll go, Miss Lum!' and, keen not to be left out, Josie and Melanie were soon heading for the door too.

'Oh, golly! So many of you!' gasped Miss Lum. 'I'd better go with you! And not in costume, Rachel! At least put your dressing gown on over the top, dear!'

Two minutes later, the room had emptied of everyone except Pippa, Luci, Sadie and me.

'Are you sure you don't want some orange?' Miss Lum had asked us, before disappearing herself.

I'd shaken my head vehemently though Miss Lum was still refusing to look my way.

'No, thank you, Miss Lum,' Sadie had added.

'Very well. I can trust you to behave yourselves while I'm gone, can't I?'

Sadie, Luci and Pippa had nodded vigorously, and Miss Lum had disappeared, pulling the door to behind her.

'Sorry,' I said to the others now. 'I just couldn't face it.'

'Don't worry,' said Pippa. 'I've had enough of Josie Wells's screeching for one evening, I can tell you.'

Just then, there was a sharp rapping on the door.

'Come in,' said Sadie.

It opened, and one of the theatre staff – a stage hand – appeared, dressed from head to foot in black, and looking far from pleased. He was holding my pointe shoes.

'Is one of you,' he turned the shoes over, to read the name on the bottom, 'Gabri–'

'Me–' I interrupted quickly. 'They're mine.' I stepped forward.

Unceremoniously, he dumped the shoes in my

outstretched hands and looked at me crossly. 'I found them in the prop cupboard,' he said. 'What the hell were they doing in there? I don't have the time to waste running up and down stairs after stupid, careless little girls.' He glared at me. I blushed and looked down.

'Sorry –' I began.

'So you ought to be,' he snapped. 'I should have just chucked them, that's what I should have done. In the nearest bin. Too soft, I am. Far too soft!' He reached for the doorhandle again. 'But if I find any another time' – he looked round at the four of us – 'you can be sure that's exactly where they'll end up!'

The door slammed behind him. For a moment, there was dead silence.

Then, 'The *prop* cupboard?' said Luci incredulously.

I shook my head. 'I haven't even set foot in there since we got to the theatre.'

'Weird!' said Sadie. 'Spooky!' She shivered.

'It's not spooky at all,' said Pippa. 'It's quite simple – someone put them in there.'

'Someone? Guy Jenkins, you mean,' said Luci.

'Hang on!' Pippa held up her hand. 'The prop cupboard, did that man say?'

Everyone nodded at her. Pippa frowned.

'What? What?' Luci grabbed hold of Pippa in frustration, looking ready to shake the words out of her.

Pippa pulled herself free, and crossed the dressing room, her forehead furrowed in thought. 'It's just –'

She turned to face us. 'I could have sworn –'

'Yes?'

'I could have sworn I saw Mary-Beth coming out of the prop cupboard yesterday, just before we went on for "Dreamers".'

'Mary-Beth *Lacey*?' asked Sadie.

'No – one of the other nine Mary-Beths in our year,' said Luci sarcastically. 'Who do you think? Oh, sorry, Sadie,' she added, as Sadie looked at her, offended.

'Yes, Mary-Beth Lacey,' said Pippa. 'I thought at the time it was an odd place for her to be snooping around in. None of us have any reason to go there that I can think of –'

'Maybe she's in league with Guy!' said Luci. 'I can't think for the life of me why – but there's only one way to find out.' She ran to the door. 'Come on! What are you lot waiting for? We've got to talk to her!'

Mary-Beth had gone down to the Green Room for squash with the others. But when Luci, Pippa, Sadie and I looked in there, we couldn't see her.

'Where's Mary-Beth?' asked Luci, grabbing the nearest person.

It was Rachel Cooper. 'Oh,' she said vaguely, 'I think she's gone to the loo.'

'Right!' Luci spun round with a determined look in her eyes.

'Hang on!' I grabbed her arm. 'We can't go and winkle her out of there.'

'We most certainly can,' said Luci fiercely, and, without waiting for further argument, she stumped back along the passageway.

'What are you going to do – look under the cubicle doors?' asked Sadie nervously, as we followed behind.

'Wait for her,' said Luci, her chin jutting forwards defiantly. 'It's like a stake-out.'

In fact, we didn't have to wait at all. As we came up to the ladies', Mary-Beth was just coming out.

When she spotted the four of us, marching determinedly towards her in formation, a look of confusion crossed her face, swiftly followed by one of unmistakeable fear. I usually try to think the best of people, but even I had to admit she looked pretty guilty about *something*.

'Mary-Beth!' called Luci, as we saw her stop, and turn, as if to go back the way she'd come.

'I – I've just remembered,' she said, gesturing behind her. 'I mean – I've forgotten–'

'Now, hold on a minute,' said Luci, taking a firm hold of her elbow. 'We want a word with you.'

'Me? Why?' Mary-Beth was white as a sheet, and her chin was already trembling.

'Hang on.' Sadie looked at Luci. 'We can't talk out here, can we? Why not go in there.' She pointed at the ladies' door. 'It's more private.'

'Good thinking,' said Luci smartly. 'Come on, Mary-Beth. Oh, and don't look so wobbly for goodness' sake. We only want to talk to you – we're not going to hurt you –'

At the very idea, Mary-Beth let out a little wail. But she did come with us even so, letting Luci pull her back through the door without any resistance.

Nineteen

'Now,' Luci flapped a hand at Sadie, indicating she should shut the door. She did so – checking both ways in the corridor outside for good measure.

'I've got to go and get my costume on for "Flowers",' said Mary-Beth, starting up from the seat Luci had plonked her in. It was the only chair in the ladies' – the rest of us had had to perch on the edge of the washbasins.

Luci put her hands on Mary-Beth's shoulders and gently pressed her down again. 'That can wait,' she said. 'There's time. We've got to get ready, too, so we're not likely to forget, are we?'

Mary-Beth swallowed hard.

Luci turned her head. 'OK – Pippa?'

'Mary-Beth.' Pippa cleared her throat. 'Yesterday, I saw you coming out of the prop store room. Yesterday, Ella's pointe shoes went missing. Today, they were found *in* the prop store room.'

'I didn't take them!' burst out Mary-Beth.

'OK, OK,' said Luci soothingly. 'Someone else took them, then, and gave them to you?'

Mary-Beth looked up at her in confusion.

Luci pushed herself off the basin and crouched at Mary-Beth's feet. 'Come on,' she said. 'We know it was Guy. He made you put the shoes in the store room, didn't he?'

'Guy?' said Mary-Beth. 'No! I never told anyone – oh!' She clapped a hand over her mouth.

'Told anyone what?' said Sadie, next to me. 'It *was* you, then!'

Mary-Beth looked desperately from one to another of our faces. Then she hung her head. 'OK, I – I –'

But no more words came out, because the next moment, Mary-Beth burst into floods of tears. Gale after gale of sobbing shook her as she rocked back and forth on her chair.

I couldn't leave her to cry like that – I started forward and put my arm round her.

Luci, still crouching next to me, looked up into Mary-Beth's red face.

'Was it you? Was it?' she repeated, gently but insistently. 'Mary-Beth, we have to know. Did you put the notes in with Ella's exam papers? Did you send the note to Guy? Mary-Beth –'

For a moment, it seemed as if the crying would never stop enough for Mary-Beth to say another word, but at last the torrent subsided and, wiping her nose with the back of her hand and sniffing loudly, Mary-Beth hiccoughed: 'Yes. Yes, it was me – it was all me –'

And then the crying began again.

I sat back on my heels, staring at her. I could hardly take it in, even now she'd admitted it, right here in front of me. What had I ever done to Mary-Beth to make her hate me that much? Nothing that I could think of, however hard I racked my brains.

'Why?' I said to Mary-Beth. 'Why?'

Mary-Beth hiccoughed again. 'You – you know when you said you knew what I felt like, having to leave this school?'

I nodded.

'Well, you didn't – but I *wanted* you to.' Suddenly her face had become twisted with bitterness and anger. 'You were the opposite of me. Everything was so perfect in your life–'

'*Perfect*?'

Mary-Beth waved her hand at me. 'Look at you! You even look perfect! And you're the best dancer in our year.'

I thought I heard a grunt from Pippa then, but Mary-Beth went on:

'All the teachers love you. They think you're so *nice,* so *hard-working.*'

'That's because she is!' said Luci fiercely.

'It's not fair!' wailed Mary-Beth.

'Well, how was stopping Ella getting the scholarship going to help you, eh?' said Sadie. 'You wouldn't be allowed to stay, you know.'

'I know that.' Mary-Beth's shoulders drooped. 'It wasn't going to help at all. I was just so – so angry and jealous. I didn't think. I – I guess it got a bit out of hand.'

'Out of hand?' Luci stood up in disgust. 'You set out to ruin Ella's chance of a great career! She's got to leave because of you, you know!'

'No – they'll never chuck you out, Ella.' Mary-Beth shook her head earnestly. 'That's the one thing I was always certain of. You're too good. I – I just wanted you to worry for a bit – but they'll never let you go.'

'Oh, yes they will,' I said bitterly. Mary-Beth looked at me. I nodded. 'They *are*. Miss Stretton said I wasn't the sort of girl the Evanova School wanted to keep, no matter what my dancing was like.'

'Really?' A look of horror flooded on to Mary-Beth's face.

'So you see,' said Pippa crisply. 'You'll just have to go to Miss Stretton and tell her the truth, won't you?'

'Miss Stretton?' Mary-Beth's horror changed to panic. 'No! I couldn't–'

Luci started forward and grabbed her wrist. 'It's the only way to stop them chucking Ella out!' she shouted. 'And what have you got to lose, eh? You're leaving anyway!' She flung Mary-Beth's arm down again.

Mary-Beth nodded. 'I will. I will go to Miss Stretton. But, oh' – she clutched Luci's hand again – 'will you all come with me? Please? I'm scared!'

Luci shook her head at this and half-smiled. 'OK then. First thing tomorrow –'

Suddenly Sadie yelped. 'Listen!' she said, nodding towards the tannoy. The orchestra was striking up a new piece of music.

We listened. 'It's that dance the Third Years do right before "Flowers"!' said Sadie, rushing to the door. 'We've got to get there in two seconds flat!'

We raced after her. In the doorway, I turned back.

Mary-Beth was still on the chair where we'd left her, looking dazed.

I ran over and grabbed her by both hands, hauling her up. 'Come on, Mary-Beth! Come *on*!'

The applause was thunderous. The audience were all on their feet, and had turned to face Madame's box. Everyone in the circle and the gods was stamping so much I thought the whole auditorium was going to collapse. And in the middle of it all, with a spotlight trained on her, Madame was beaming at everyone, waving one gnarled hand regally and nodding to the audience, and to us, the dancers on stage.

'Look!' hissed Sadie next to me, out of the corner of her smile. 'Behind Madame in the box – it's Lily Dempsey!'

I looked – and yes, it was. An elegant young woman with a face I knew so well, from the hundreds of photographs I'd pored over. But I'd never seen her out of costume before. She was wearing a plain black dress with a scoop neck, and something sparkling at her throat. She looked stunning.

I was still gazing at her when the orchestra struck up, and everyone – performers and spectators – sang 'Happy Birthday' to Madame.

The stage was full, with every pupil who'd performed tonight crowded on to it, still in costume. We'd taken our bows already. And there I was in the middle of the crush, singing and cheering and clapping with the best of them.

Nothing had changed; Guy still had the scholarship, and I still had to leave the Evanova School – but at least my name would be cleared.

I wanted Miss Stretton and Miss Latimer to know that I hadn't cheated. That I hadn't sent that letter – and I wanted Guy to know, too.

Twenty

'The letter to Guy Jenkins,' Mary-Beth said, her voice hardly louder than a whisper. 'I sent it.'

Miss Stretton's eyebrows raised themselves one notch, but she said nothing.

Mary-Beth cleared her throat. 'And – before that, I took some of Ella's notes and put a page in with the history exam papers – so it would look like she cheated.'

Miss Stretton narrowed her eyes and pointed round at Luci, Sadie, Pippa and me. 'These girls have persuaded you to say this, Mary-Beth, I suppose? They have bullied you into it –'

'No!' Mary-Beth turned to me in anguish, and then looked back at Miss Stretton.

Miss Stretton pursed her lips. 'We shall see,' she said. 'I would like to speak to you alone for a moment, Mary-Beth. The rest of you may leave.'

'But–' Luci began.

'Out!' snapped Miss Stretton. 'Now!'

'Why do they have to make these doors so thick?' said Luci, putting her ear to the crack. She paused, then shook her head. 'Can't hear a thing.'

My teeth were chattering. Would Mary-Beth stick to what she had told us? Would Miss Stretton try to persuade her out of it? All of a sudden, everything seemed to be hanging by a thread.

At last, Luci sprang back from the door, and the next second it opened. Mary-Beth came out, white as a sheet, and then Miss Stretton appeared. 'The rest of you may come in now,' she said.

Miss Stretton settled herself back in her chair as Pippa closed the door and stepped forward, level with the rest of us, in a line before the large desk.

'I am very glad that this matter has been cleared up,' said Miss Stretton. Her bony fingers were pulling at her collar in a fidgety manner. 'And – um – I regret that I misjudged you, Gabriella,' she said hurriedly, looking at a spot somewhere just past my left ear.

'That's not much use now, is it?' muttered Luci beside me.

'What was that?' said Miss Stretton, looking at her severely.

'I said –' Luci took a gulp for courage. 'I said that it's no good now, Miss Stretton. Ella didn't get that scholarship, so she still has to leave the school, doesn't she?'

'Yes, well.' Miss Stretton paused. 'I had been trying to dissuade him from it – but now I see no reason . . .' she mumbled to herself. Then she noticed our puzzled expressions. 'Perhaps,' she said briskly, shuffling the papers on her desk, 'perhaps that matter is not entirely closed.'

I looked at her quickly. But she didn't say any more.

'You may go now, girls,' she said, pulling her lips into a tight smile.

Luci seemed to be about to burst with curiosity. She glanced at me, then looked back to Miss Stretton. 'What–'

'You may *go* now,' Miss Stretton repeated.

Reluctantly, we did as we were told.

'Perhaps that matter is not entirely closed.'

Those words haunted me, swirling round and round my brain for the rest of the day.

'They're going to let you stay, I just know they are!' Sadie said that evening, bouncing up and down on my bed.

Luci was sitting next to her, swinging her feet thoughtfully. She never trusted Miss Stretton an inch, and though she wasn't saying anything, I knew she wasn't so sure Sadie was right.

'What can they do?' I said. 'The scholarship funds have been used up – and they can't very well kick Guy out in favour of me, can they? It wouldn't be right. He deserved that scholarship anyway.'

'So did you,' began Pippa. But that moment, Miss Lum stuck her head round the door. It was so wonderful to see her warm smile turned on me again, just like old times.

'Sadie! Luci!' she said, attempting to change her smile into a frown. 'You should be in your own room now, my dears! I want these lights off in five minutes!'

'Yes, Miss Lum.' Sadie and Luci got up, and headed for the door.

No, I thought, as I pushed my feet down under the

bedclothes – I was leaving. I had to face up to it. I should just be thankful that the truth had come out at last. And enjoy my last few days at the Evanova while I could.

Twenty-one

We were on our way to breakfast the next morning when Luci saw something that made her seize my arm and gasp. 'Oh no – look!'

'What?' Pippa, Sadie and I looked about us, confusedly.

'It's Guy,' said Luci, pointing to where he was standing further down the corridor, staring at something on a notice board.

I nodded. 'I feel really bad. For all that time we thought it was him who was doing those mean things.'

'*You* feel bad?' said Luci incredulously. 'It was *me* that went and blew my mouth off at him about it.' She winced. 'I was so convinced it was him. I dread to think what I said . . . Oh, let's turn back! I can't walk past.'

Sadie laughed. 'You mean you're going to spend the rest of your time at this school trying to avoid him? That's going to be a bit tricky. Particularly since we've got English first thing after ballet. And then there's History.'

'OK, OK. I'll hack it.' Luci turned again to face the way we were going.

'Why don't you' – Sadie nudged her – 'go and talk to him about it?'

'What do you mean "talk to him"? Oh no –' Luci

drew back, realising what Sadie was getting at. 'You mean apologise, right? No way! Me? Say sorry to *Guy Jenkins*?'

'You *were* in the wrong,' pointed out Pippa helpfully.

I put my hand on Luci's shoulder. '*I* should apologise,' I said firmly. 'It was all because of me in the first place.' I started forward away from the others, but Luci yanked me back.

'No, you don't!' she said. 'I'm doing it.'

She stopped short, staring in Guy's direction. The rest of us followed her gaze – in time to see Guy striding purposefully towards us.

'Hi,' he said, drawing to a halt and looking suddenly awkward. He scratched his cheek and fixed his eyes on the floor.

'Er – hi,' I said. My three friends seemed to have been struck dumb.

Guy stood for a minute, shifting his weight from foot to foot. 'Oh, yeah,' he said at last. 'Ella, I – just wanted to say I heard it was Mary-Beth who sent that note. So I shouldn't have–'

'It's OK,' I said quickly. 'We shouldn't have accused you about the exams and–'

'It was my fault!' broke in Luci suddenly. 'Completely. Entirely.' With what seemed like an enormous effort, she looked Guy straight in the face. 'Mine.'

There was a pause. Then Luci gave a sort of throat-clearing cough. But I could have sworn I heard the word 'sorry' in the middle of it somewhere.

Guy nodded. 'It's cool,' he said. Then he turned on his heel and headed off down the corridor.

Luci collapsed on me in mock exhaustion. 'Give me three *allegro* classes back to back!' she hissed. 'Give me a whole day's non-stop pointe work! I don't care! Just never, *ever* put me through the pain of apologising to Guy Jenkins again!'

'Come on!' I laughed, pushing her upright. 'It could be the beginning of a beautiful friendship.'

I can't even describe the face Luci made then. Just think of the Chamber of Horrors.

Only worse.

Twenty-two

Miss Latimer set down her small bag and turned to the class. We were lined up at the barre as usual, ready for *pliés*.

'Gabriella,' Miss Latimer said, smiling at me for the first time in weeks. 'Madame wishes to see you. Straight away.'

I hesitated. Then I ran to the corner to pick up my pointe shoes and headed for the door. Three faces grinned at me as I passed.

Although it was a warm morning, I found myself shivering as I hurried along the corridor towards Madame's apartment.

When I reached the door, I paused for a moment. Then I raised my hand, and knocked.

'Come in!' said a sharp voice.

I opened the door and stepped into Madame's private sitting room – a place I'd been just once before, at the beginning of my very first term at the Evanova.

The room had an atmosphere quite different from the classrooms and offices of the rest of the school. On my left, there was a stately marble fireplace flanked by two large windows, each with curtains that draped right to the floor. Opposite, one entire wall of the room was covered with shelves upon shelves of old books, and I was surprised to see there, instead of

Madame in her wheelchair, a big bulky figure of a man standing looking up at the volumes.

'Ah, Gabriella!' But it was Madame's voice that spoke, and for a moment I couldn't see where it was coming from. Then, with a whirring sound, she moved her chair from the shadows of the far corner into the centre of the room.

'Good morning, Madame,' I said hurriedly, bobbing a small curtsey.

'Gabriella,' Madame said again. 'I would like you to meet Mr Bernard Schindenberg.'

At this, the man by the bookshelves turned. He must have been a bit older than Papa, perhaps – but with dark bushy eyebrows, and big, square hands. He strode towards me now, one of these hands stuck out in front of him. I was so amazed that at first I didn't realise what I was supposed to do.

'Oh –' I put out my hand at last. It was like shaking hands with a bear. I curtsied again, and that made Mr Schindenberg laugh – a deep rumbly bubbling in his chest.

'Sit down, Gabriella.' Madame indicated a chair by the fireplace. Mr Schindenberg came and sat in another one, nearer to Madame.

I perched on the edge of the chair. It was a large, winged leather chair and it made me feel very small.

'Mr Schindenberg,' began Madame crisply, nodding politely in his direction, 'has made a kind offer, Gabriella. An extremely kind offer. And – since you have now been cleared of those unfortunate accusations' – she stopped and, with a wave of her hand, seemed to dismiss the subject – 'Miss Stretton tells me she now has no objections to you accepting it. The offer is to pay your school fees for the rest of your time with us.'

'Next year's – next year's fees?' I said hesitantly, hardly able to believe my ears.

Mr Schindenberg nodded. 'And the year after that – and the one after that too!' he said, in a deep American voice. 'I believe in encouraging talent, Gabriella. So I'd like to see you through the school, right until you graduate. If it's acceptable to you and your parents, that is.'

I felt like laughing and crying – both at once. 'Yes! I mean, I'm sure Mamma and Papa . . . Oh, I – I – don't know what to say!'

Madame tapped the tips of her fingers together. 'You would do well to *thank* Mr Schindenberg, Gabriella,' she said.

'Oh, yes of course.' I felt myself blushing. 'Thank you, Mr Schindenberg. Thank you *so* much. I can't tell you–'

'It's my pleasure, Gabriella.' Mr Schindenberg laughed. 'Now, Miss Evanova,' he turned to Madame, 'may I suggest that Gabriella and I could perhaps take a turn of your beautiful grounds together?' He waved a hand towards the window. 'I could explain the background of what must be for her a rather surprising piece of news.'

Madame nodded. 'Certainly, Mr Schindenberg.

Gabriella, run and get changed quickly into your outdoor clothes.'

'Yes, Madame.' I stood up, curtsied again, and flew to the door.

'My, it's a beautiful school you have here,' said Mr Schindenberg fifteen minutes later, as we walked side by side along the gravel path that runs between the flowerbeds in a wide ring, right round the school building.

I took a sideways glance at him. He looked vaguely familiar, though I couldn't think why. It was weird – as if I'd dreamt him or something. I racked my brains. Had he something to do with the British National Ballet production we'd all been in at Christmas? No – that didn't seem to fit.

He was wearing a great big black overcoat, made of some thick material that looked as if he could take it off and it would still stand up on its own. He was carrying a black shiny stick, too, though he didn't seem to have any trouble walking – he just swung the stick out in front of him as he strode.

'When I said I was coming over to England,' Mr Schindenberg went on, 'my sister said I simply had to visit The Evanova School. And when I saw you dancing in the dress rehearsal for your gala show, it was no surprise to me that you were the Gabriella Bruni she had talked about. "That little girl is a natural, Bernard," she'd said to me.'

'Your sister?'

Mr Schindenberg nodded. 'Christine Schindenberg Weller. I believe you met her and her husband Arnold while they were on holiday in Italy?'

Of course! The couple who'd been staying at Nonna's back at Easter. And that's who Mr Schindenberg reminded me of – the woman with the big round glasses! I could see the likeness quiet clearly now – they both had the same smily faces.

Mr Schindenberg was laughing. My shock and surprise must have been obvious.

'Coincidence, huh?' he rumbled. 'Well, stranger things have happened!' He seemed to consider this thought for a moment, and then went on, 'I've been supporting ballet in the States for many years. But I've been wanting to do something here too for a long time now. My mother was English, you see. She was born in Stratford-upon-Avon. Like William Shakespeare!' And Mr Schindenberg chuckled again.

'Now,' he inclined his head politely, 'are there any questions you'd like to ask me?'

I nodded. 'There is something . . .' I hesitated. 'Mr Schindenberg –'

'Call me Bernard,' he said.

'Bernard –' It sounded funny to call such a stately and important-looking person by his first name. 'It's a bit of a strange request, actually. It's just that – well, my dad's really proud about money. He's got this idea that you should help yourself, not take hand-outs from anyone –' I stopped and bit my lip. Papa's ideas sounded really rude now I was repeating them to someone who'd made such a kind offer.

'I think I know what you're telling me,' said Bernard, nodding gravely. 'Is there anything I can do to make it easier for your father to accept my help?'

'Well – I think so,' I said. 'If you called it "The Schindenberg Scholarship", or something, it would make it sound more official . . .'

I looked up at Bernard anxiously to see how he would react.

Bernard went on walking, his forehead crinkled up in thought. 'The Schindenberg Scholarship,' he repeated to himself. Then he smiled at me. 'Doesn't sound bad, does it?' Then he put one heavy hand on my shoulder. 'Well, Gabriella. I'll speak to Miss Evanova about that, and see what I can do.'

Soon we were back at the front entrance of the school again, and I led the way inside.

'Could you direct me back to Miss Evanova's room?' asked Bernard. 'I still haven't quite gotten the hang of the layout of this building.'

'Of course,' I said quickly. 'I'll take you.'

As we came round the corner into the Dance Wing, we met Luci, Sadie and Pippa, changed after their ballet lesson, coming the other way.

'Hey Ella – oh!' Luci pulled herself up sharply when she saw Bernard. 'I'm sorry, I–'

'No need to apologise, my dear,' he rumbled. 'I am pleased to meet any friends of Gabriella's.'

Luci looked at me in astonishment.

'These are my three best friends in the world!' I

said. 'Luci Simpson, Sadie Marsh, and Pippa James.'

'Delighted,' said Bernard, shaking hands with each in turn. Then he frowned. 'Tell me – did you four dance together in that modern piece in the gala? Now what was it called?'

' "Dreamers"?' suggested Luci.

'That's it!' Bernard beamed. 'I'm right then?'

'You are, sir,' said Luci. 'I choreographed it myself.'

'Then let me shake you by the hand once more!' said Bernard, proffering his hand again. 'I was saying to Miss Evanova just earlier this morning what a startling piece I thought it was. And I see a great number of ballet performances, my dear.'

'Thank you, sir,' said Luci, beaming, 'I hope to become a choreographer one day.'

'Amongst other things,' said Pippa, nudging her.

'Do you now?' Bernard's eyebrows shot up.

For a moment Luci's smile faltered. 'Is – is that not a good idea?' she said.

'No, no! Quite the opposite!' Bernard put a hand to his chin. 'I was simply thinking. You see, there's a ballet academy I know of in the States that runs a summer school for young choreographers.'

Luci's eyes widened. 'Really?'

'It's in L.A., if my memory serves me right . . .'

'Los Angeles?' said Luci. 'Isn't that where Hollywood is?'

Bernard nodded. 'Keen to see some film stars, are you?'

Luci clapped her hands together. 'My step-dad's got

a job out there this summer. I could go with him!'

'Sounds like it was meant to be!' chuckled Bernard. 'I'll have a word with the principal when I get back home. But for now' – he gave a small bow – 'I'm afraid I must go. Gabriella?'

'Oh, yes,' I said. 'Madame's apartment isn't far from here. Follow me.'

As Bernard and I walked on down the corridor, I glanced back, and saw Luci, Sadie and Pippa still standing where we had left them, staring after us in shock.

Twenty-three

'Hey, hey, hey! Start again! You met this couple in Italy?' Luci grabbed my hands and dragged me to sit next to her on Pippa's bed.

'At Easter – they were staying at my grandma's little hotel.'

'And he's the brother of the woman,' said Pippa, still trying to get it straight.

'That's right.'

'And he just turns out to be some rich guy who goes around funding ballet students?' Luci shook her head in amazement.

'Students and companies and theatres, I think. All sorts.'

'Wow! Ella, it's incredible.' Sadie laughed.

'I know.' I flopped back against the wall. 'I can hardly believe it myself!'

'So is he the same man you saw Miss Stretton with at the dress rehearsal?' Sadie asked Luci.

'Jeepers, I'd forgotten that! You're dead right! It all fits in, now!'

Just then there was a knock at the door. It opened straight away, and Miss Lum's face appeared.

'Dear girls! I have just received the strangest message for you! A Mr' – she looked down at the card she was holding in her hand – 'Bernard Schin – Schinden –'

'Schindenberg?' offered Sadie.

'Thank you, my dear,' Miss Lum nodded. 'Well, he has invited all four of you to tea with him this Sunday afternoon, at the Cedar Tea Rooms in Wittingham. Apparently, Miss Stretton has given her permission for a taxi to pick you up at the school gates at a quarter to four – if you want to go, that is.'

'Do we?' said Luci, bouncing up and down on her bed.

'Yes, please!' we chorused together.

'Well, aren't you the lucky ones, dear hearts?' Miss Lum beamed at us fondly and disappeared again, shutting the door.

'Yes,' I sighed, looking round at my three friends. 'Yes, I really think we are.'